NOC CITY

BOOK ONE

PENN CASSIDY

Noc City
Book One
Penn Cassidy

Copyright © 2020 Penn Cassidy

Printed in the United States of America
First Printing, 2020

Editing: Meghan Leigh Daigle - Bookish Dreams Editing
Formatting: Inked Imagination Services

CONTENTS

DISCLAIMER

This is a DARK reverse harem book. There's a LOT of blood, sex, MM, and swears, not to mention references to suicide, abuse, and trauma. This is your fair warning, so if you say you like dark romance...please understand that this is a DARK ROMANCE.

P.S. If you are in any way related to me...I urge you to reconsider this read, or else our family dinners are about to get weird.

ABOUT NOC CITY

They call me the Angel of Noc City, but it's all a lie. The cameras see what they want to see as my father spins half truths and dangerous propaganda.

Darklings are dangerous. Monstrous. Unholy. They're a threat to humans everywhere, and they need to be destroyed, despite the decades of peace.

But what happens when Noc City's poster girl discovers she's one of the monsters they fear? I can tell you what happens.

Chaos. Fear. War.

I thought death was my only way out. Sweet, dark oblivion. But I was wrong. The way out might just be through a room of chains, blood, and cravings...of sex, pain, and betrayal. My way out of this hell might rest in the hands of the most dangerous creatures Noc City's ever known.

SPOTIFY PLAYLIST

https://open.spotify.com/playlist/399AVc6tHpGzfE2i6OjVqh?
si=Vc3vFrgqRCqeKazHvmYxSQ

PROLOGUE

"*J*ust tell me what you need to know," I said breathlessly. "It's what you brought me here for, right?" I was still tied to the wall hours later.

I must've fallen asleep at some point, because when I came to, one of the hooded men was standing in the center of the room, staring at me with his arms crossed over his chest. I wondered how long he'd been here, watching me sleep. Once again, I marveled at the size of him. He was all broad shoulders, wide stance, and thick arms.

"You realize I have every reason to despise him, right?" I gave him a dubious stare. "Probably even more than you do..."

He loosed something that sounded like a huff or a snort, shaking his head. I felt a sliver of satisfaction that I'd been able to coax a small reaction from him at all. Surprising me, he said, "I highly doubt that, Miss Harker."

I chuckled darkly. "Miss Harker? A bit formal for a hostage situation, don't you think?"

His shoulders dropped ever so slightly, and I imagined he was grinning under that mask. I was pushing my luck with these guys, but the longer they held me here, the more I thought about *it objectively. I truly didn't think they wanted to cause me real pain for the sake of pain itself. They needed me for something and were simply using the most efficient way of going about achieving it.*

"Ryan Harker has something of mine, and I want it back," the man said finally.

Okay...I was not expecting that. "What does he have?" I asked.

"Doesn't matter right now."

"I think it does," I snapped, suddenly even more irritated than before. "You kidnapped me, tied me up like an animal, and drank my blood without my consent. You don't think I at least deserve to know why? You know my biggest secret. I think I'm entitled to something."

The man came closer, taking slow, deliberate steps. I felt my stomach tighten as he came within touching distance, looming over me like a shadow. I could see my angry brown eyes in the reflection of the mirror mask. I looked paler than ever, and there were dark circles under my eyes—a product of the blood loss, no doubt.

"Tell me, Miss Harker..." He came closer, uncomfortably so. I wondered if he could hear my heart racing. Taking a gloved finger, he ran it down the side of my face, trailing it downward towards my collar bone. "Has the bloodlust started yet?" My breath caught as he clicked his tongue. "The cravings can be... intense, to put it mildly."

Turning my face away, I clamped my mouth shut. At the mention of bloodlust, I could feel a stinging in my gums, reminding me of the last time I nearly lost control. I remembered the wild feeling of desperation in that crowd at Rue. I remembered my eyes in that bathroom mirror, glossing over in black and red, tiny spidery veins snaking through my skin. I was a monster. Unhinged. Thirsty.

"There she is..." His thumb brushed my throat, and he laid his palm on the side of my neck. I gulped hard as he brought his face closer. "Have you ever indulged, Serenity?" He said my name like he knew me, and I swear my pussy throbbed. My fangs were fully extended now. "No, you wouldn't have, would you? Not the Angel of Noc City."

"Get your hands off of me," I gritted out, trying to keep my fangs concealed. Despite my paleness, I knew my cheeks were turning scarlett. I wasn't embarrassed, per se. I was ashamed. The power his words had over my body made me sick.

"Why don't you tell me what you really want, little dhampir?" he cooed, and the voice box crackled, sending a thrill through my body. "Did you know dhampirs can survive off the blood of both humans and vampires?"

My heart gave a painful lurch. No, I hadn't known that. Why would I?

I could imagine he was grinning under the mask now, knowing he had my attention. He backed away slightly, but instead of leaving, he made a show of slowly pulling off his gloves. Strong pale hands were revealed, each finger holding a different ring with weird, unfamiliar symbols etched into them. I recognized only one, though I'm sure the thought didn't cross his mind. I stared at the symbol of the Nocturne Coven on his middle finger. It was the shape of an upside down cross with a snake coiled up the center. I was right. I knew exactly who my captor was.

I watched in fascination as he transformed his pointer finger into a claw. His nail lengthened to a lethal point, and he brought it to the opposite wrist.

"They say a dhampir's first taste of vampire blood is sweeter than ambrosia. They say it's better than the best fuck you'll ever have and then some." I could feel his stare down to my bones as he added, "Care to test that theory?"

CHAPTER 1
SERENITY

*H*is smile was too wide. White teeth glared in the midday sun like a toothpaste commercial. The golden hair, the fair, peachy skin, and the laugh lines around those twinkling blue eyes mocked me. My stomach rolled, threatening to send its contents over the back of my father's four-thousand-dollar Armani suit. The mental image was almost enough to bring a grin to my lips. Almost.

It was too bright out, and my eyes were already stinging. The sun was turning my skin pink, and my mouth had never been so dry. I hated the oppressive heat of the summer. I hated sweating and squinting and shifting around uncomfortably, knowing relief wouldn't come for a while yet. My mother's hand in mine was the only thing anchoring me to the spot, even though I felt like ripping mine away and brushing my palm off on my expensive dress. I could feel her diamond rings against my skin and the slick of sweat beading on her palm.

Her serene smile was as fake as the bland expression on my face. The crowd watched and waited, laughing politely every time Senator Ryan Harker, my father, cracked an unfunny joke. It was mostly humans in this crowd— surprise, surprise—but it was hard to tell sometimes. I thought I'd spotted several shifters towards the back of the crowd earlier, but the grassy expanse in front of the museum steps was too packed with humans now to tell anyone apart.

My father's voice was grating and made my stomach roll. He didn't even sound like himself up there. He sounded happy, jovial even, but it was all a ruse. He was charismatic and handsome when he wanted to be. An all-American man with the world in his palm—the same palm I could still feel on my cheek like it was burning down to the muscle. My makeup artist did a wonderful job covering it up for me. His college ring had caught my left cheek, slicing a little too deep to really call it a scratch. The woman had simply *tsked*, but I could see the turmoil in her worried eyes every time she was forced to hold her tongue for the sake of her job. On camera, I probably appeared soft, unblemished, plucked, and polished to within an inch of my life—all the things he needed me to be for his adoring fans.

I missed the entire last half of his speech, eyes glazing over and staring at nothing in particular. Honestly, I didn't need to hear it to know what he was blathering on about. The usual rhetoric. It was always more of the same shit, and people just ate it right up. I could hear him right now, spewing the same garbage as usual—humans were the superior race, darklings were second class citizens and a threat to god fearing humans everywhere. The usual hatred and malice, nothing new. I had to stand up here and smile like I didn't feel like throwing up every time he opened his mouth.

The roar of the crowd had my focus snapping back into

place. They clapped for my father, chanting his name over and over again like some kind of cult following. I had no idea how long I'd been tapped out for, but it was happening more and more these days. Sometimes, I'd feel myself zoning out when I needed to be paying attention and pretending to be a loyal member of the Harker family. My eyes would unfocus and my mind would wander, only to clear however many moments later, usually to find my father glaring at me with those twinkling eyes that promised pain when the cameras were gone.

My mother squeezed my hand once before letting go. She left my side and joined my father at the podium, placing a delicate hand on his shoulder. She looked perfect today. The picture of a beautiful human housewife. White blonde hair that she passed down to me flowed over her shoulders in delicate waves. Her fitted cream-colored suit was pressed and went perfectly with her nude Prada pumps. Flawless. Perfect. Elodie Harker was perfect.

My father slung an arm around her casually, but I could tell his fingers on her hip were digging in deep enough to leave a bruise later. It was a good thing her stylist put her in pantsuits most of the time, because the media would be in nothing less than a frenzy at the sight of the black and blue legs I knew she was hiding underneath that silk and cashmere. It was a pity she lost her backbone somewhere along the way, but that thought implied she had one to begin with, which was doubtful.

It was my turn now. Time to play pretend for a little while longer. To play the part he expected me to play. I'd do it. For her, I'd do it. I walked to his other side, plastering a fake smile on my face. I even showed some teeth today for a little razzle dazzle. The muscles around my lips were straining and burning, fighting a losing battle once again.

His arm came up around my shoulders, and it was all I could do to keep the flinch inside. That hand felt like slime coating my now very sunburned skin. His fingers dug into my bicep, pressing down hard enough to force a brighter smile out of me. It was a warning—play the doting, flawless angel of a daughter for the world to fall in love with. Pretend we were the perfect nuclear family.

But we weren't. Not at all. We were missing one. Sean's absence was a heavy weight at my side. Even after nearly a full twelve months, I could feel my fingers twitching to reach for my older brother, itching to grasp his hand and squeeze. Sean and I had a code. It was something we'd made up when we were toddlers and our parents wanted us to keep our mouths shut around their politician friends. One squeeze for *I'm here*. Two squeezes for *this is stupid*, three squeezes for *I love you*.

My eyes burned so badly, I had to pretend it was the glare of the setting sun. I missed Sean so much it made me sick sometimes. Even sicker than the feel of my father's grip on my shoulder. We waved and smiled for the crowd of dumbass human supporters. Most of them were holding up signs with our last name on it. *Harker for Senator.* Again, I should say. He'd been state senator for years, always running unopposed, and I saw no foreseeable end to the madness. He was the beloved voice of the humans in Noc City and the surrounding territories of our home state. This was the last place on Earth this man should have any control over. If only these smiling sheep knew what lurked beneath that toothpaste grin.

They were just like him though, those who flocked to these events—humans who thought the world would be better off without the darklings. Bigots, as I liked to call them. Racists who didn't deserve the smiles they wore or the comfortable jobs and lavish homes paid for with blood money. My father was an icon for these people and human districts stretching statewide. Ryan Harker was their leader, and in turn, so was I in a sense. My face was plastered on pamphlets, posters, television, and social media, right there alongside the smiling tyrant.

His fingers began digging into my arm even harder than before, and his fingernails were sharp, burning into my sun sensitive skin. I had to keep smiling, pretending everything was perfect. Pretending I didn't want to switch places with Sean every single day.

When our time was up, I was ushered off the stage by our security detail. I walked fast but still manageable, trying to avoid any unnecessary touching. Sometimes those guys got a bit handsy, and for twelve months now, my temper had run hot. My mother and I were led around the back of the museum where the press conference was being held and shoved into a limo under the flash of cameras, while my father stayed back to pose for photos. I was used to it. The fame. The lack of privacy. I just went through the practiced steps like an emotionless doll most days, my body just going through the motions.

The cheers abruptly died down when the limousine door closed. The fake smile dropped off my face, and I immediately reached down beneath the seat to where a built-in fridge awaited and promptly threw back three healthy slugs of thick, rich wine that I'd made sure to stash there earlier. My mother just watched vacantly, her watery green eyes as dead as my soul. Sweet bliss coursed through my veins. I leaned my head back against the headrest, kicking off my heels, and shut my eyes.

"You're lucky your father can't see you right now."

"He's not my father." Snapping my eyes open, I glared at

my mother. "You made sure of that." It was a low blow, but deserving. Maybe it was wrong of me to blame her. Maybe it was stupid to be angry at the fact that I was alive. If she never had the affair in the first place, I wouldn't exist right now.

"I don't have the energy for this right now, Serenity." She pinched the bridge of her nose with manicured fingers, closing her eyes. Just like that, I could no longer feel the oppressive weight of her misplaced judgment.

"Nobody asked you to speak, *mother*," I sneered, taking two more mouthfuls of sweet red wine before closing my eyes again. I was thirsty. So fucking thirsty my throat contracted, and it was dry like I'd chewed on cotton balls. I knew I needed something other than this wine. I knew it, but I ignored it.

I didn't get why she had to be such a bitch when we were alone. I was twenty-four years old for fuck's sake. I could drink myself to death if I wanted to, and nobody could tell me otherwise. Sometimes, I wondered if that wasn't the preferable way to go. At least I could control that. Actually, I was lying to myself yet again. I couldn't get drunk. Not really. Not that I'd had much practice. I was a good girl up until twelve months ago, with good grades, a handsome boyfriend, lots of friends... Another life entirely.

It was only a hazy blink of an eye before we were pulling up to the front of our mansion. Tall black gates were flanked by brick and shrubbery, behind which a white columned monstrosity stood. Ryan Harker was a try-hard, and it was pathetic. He thought so highly of himself, but to me, it was just tacky and pathetic. I'd always hated this house, even before all the bad days. Sean and I used to pretend we were living in the White House sometimes. We'd run around the manicured lawns, laughing and teasing each other mercilessly, while our security detail frantically tried to corral us back inside. Such memories this place held...but not all of them were happy.

Spread out through the property were tall stadium lights fitted with bright UV bulbs that came on every evening at six-thirty. My father had them built out of swirling, decorative wrought iron posts to make them more palatable for company and the media, but I couldn't help but feel like I was stuck in some kind of prison. There hadn't been a vampire attack in the entire history of the city's founding. He was just a douchebag in my opinion.

I didn't wait for the driver to open my door. I was out and dashing up to the house before he had the chance to get out of the car. I was so sick of being carted around and watched every single moment of my life, of never having the opportunity to be alone. I tried to get in before anyone followed behind, but the second I opened the front door, I ran smack into a hard body.

"Whoa there, slow down." Carson placed his hands on my shoulders, and I could smell the pungent cologne wafting off his suit jacket. I suppressed a gag. "What's the rush, baby doll?"

Okay, now I really was going to gag. I hated when he called me that. Carson Badgley—human, golden boy, brown noser, and Harvard graduate. He was also, unfortunately, my boyfriend.

Carson's arm came around my shoulders, and a whiff of fresh air that blessedly wasn't laced with Versace graced my nostrils, dulling the sting in my eyes. "Let's get you a drink. You look like you need it."

I made a small sound of affirmation. He had me there, I did need a stiff drink. Or two. Or ten. Hell, just hook me up to an IV already and call it a day. It wasn't like it would do anything. Alcohol, it seemed, dissolved in my bloodstream before it had the chance to take effect. Another little perk of my...condition. I knew this because I'd tested it more than enough times since Sean was killed to be sure. According to my mental math, I should have been dead of alcohol poisoning months ago.

I was tired and just wanted to go to sleep before my father could get home, sparing me his fists and his lectures. Holding my shoes in one hand, I limped alongside Carson. He handed me a glass of amber liquid. I didn't give a shit what it was, just knocked it back, wiping my lips a moment later with the back of my hand as Carson watched with barely veiled lust in his blue eyes.

"You want to talk about it?" he asked, though he sounded bored already and uninterested.

"Shut up, Carson." Christ, his voice was grating on my last nerve already.

Setting my glass down on the bartop, I grabbed his red tie and dragged him along behind me. He came without question, not bothering to berate me for talking to him the way I had. He had one thing on his mind right now, and it was my only saving grace. Carson Badgley had a temper almost as short as my father's, and he liked very much to flex that temper any time he decided he didn't like what came out of my mouth. Which was becoming more and more frequent the less I realized I cared.

I had an entire wing of the mansion to myself, thank god for small mercies. I used to share it with Sean, back before... before the worst day of my life. For the most part, our parents left us alone as we got older. My father never had time for us, and my mother was just vacant and drunk most of the time. We'd liked it that way though. But now, the emptiness and my brother's closed bedroom door just mocked me every time I passed it.

Practically kicking my door open, I shoved Carson in my bedroom, locking us inside the darkness. The housekeeper had my fireplace running, so it was nice and warm, and Carson was already loosening the tie I'd released. He knew what was coming—it was the only reason he bothered to stop by. After the shit day I'd had, I needed a release, and Carson was the best outlet at the moment. I didn't love him, not in the slightest. Actually, I barely even liked him. I only dated him because his father was my father's closest associate and it was expected.

It was lucky Carson happened to be a feast for the eyes. I had to admit that at least, even if he had a soggy walnut for a brain. Tall, broad, blond, and fake tanned. Carson had a nice body for the personification of a piece of stale bread. You'd never guess it from the endless number of tan suits he wore.

"Come here, baby, doll." His smile was wide and lecherous, but I ignored my revulsion in favor of this growing need inside me.

"I said shut up, Carson." A dark flash of something violent passed in his eyes, but I shoved it aside for a later time.

With a swift push to his chest, he toppled to my bed easily. In seconds, my sensible navy blue wrap dress was over my head, revealing a bright crimson lace bralette and nothing else. Through the dark, I saw Carson take me in from head to toe appreciatively. I knew what I looked like. I realized the appeal I had for men, groomed to within an inch of my life at all times. From a young age, I'd been forced to get laser hair removal and keep my pale hair flowing long and touching my hips.

I was everything Carson dreamed of in a woman, so I used that to my advantage, even if some days I'd give anything to switch bodies with a hobo on the street. Anything to get out of this hell I called my life these days. Though I was sure I disgusted him to the core, Carson still salivated over my body every time we were alone, this body that I once thought was ordinary, human. I was changing more and more every week, and I knew he could see it. They all could. I could feel it every second of every day since the accident. Since that blood touched my tongue and the monster living inside of me began to wake.

Carson was pulling his dick out already. His slacks weren't even off yet, but I didn't care. I didn't need anything else, just that hard length he pumped in his palm. The last remnants of sunlight peeked through my curtains, illuminating the room with shards of sunbeams slashing through shadows and flickering firelight. Carson's cock leaked at the tip, and he used his thumb to swirl it around the engorged head. A shiver rolled through me that I couldn't suppress.

His cock was huge. It was one of the main reasons I had yet to break up with the bastard. I hated to sound so shallow, but a girl had needs. With my father being who he was, my prospects were minuscule, and it was only a matter of time before the details of my dirty truth came to light. The only thing holding this charade together was Ryan Harker's absolute need to save face and put on a show. If the world was to find out that the beautiful and perfect Elodie Harker stepped out on her marriage...well, I didn't really want to think about that right now.

Crawling onto the bed, I didn't bother giving him head. He had an army of women around to suck him off, so he didn't need me for that. I was already wet. Reaching down, I rubbed my clit back and forth, pressing down hard enough for spikes of pleasure to roll up my spine. A breathy moan slipped from my lips, and I heard Carson's answering groan. He might hate my species, but he loved what my body could make him feel. So I used it to my advantage once again, but I hated myself for it. I hated myself for a lot of things, might as well add hate fucking to the list.

Lowering my hips, I slid my pussy over his length, feeling warmth roll over me. Carson's head fell backwards, his chest rising and falling rapidly. Several curses filled the room as I began to grind in a steady rhythm that I knew drove him crazy. When I was finally ready, I rose up and wrapped my hand around the base of his cock, then slid it inside me until he bottomed out. I sat there with my eyes closed for a moment, relishing the full, warm feeling. I reached backwards and fondled his balls lightly, running my sharp nails along the sensitive skin, which prompted his hips to jolt off the bed, hitting me where I needed him. This wasn't for his pleasure at all. It was for mine. I thought about all the times this man tried to intimidate and belittle me, putting every ounce of hatred into the way I fucked him. It was the only way I could continue.

Leaning forward again, I started to move. I wasn't slow or soft. I fucked myself on his cock as if he were nothing but a toy. He was my dildo—a warm, fleshy cock for me to bounce on. He could have been anyone and it wouldn't have made a difference, but he was who I was stuck with. My cravings for physical touch were growing steadily by the day, to the point that I actually started to enjoy sex, even with somebody I loathed. Slipping my hand between my thighs as I fucked him, I rubbed my clit furiously, needing the burning release it would bring me.

I felt a stinging in my mouth as I gyrated on his dick. Staring up towards the crystal chandelier hanging from my ceiling, I felt the skin around my eyes tightening, knowing my eyes were changing color. If I looked down right now, Carson would be able to watch me lose control. He'd see the monster inside of me show her true face. He'd finish fucking me, but I'd pay for it later. My teeth burned, and my mouth went dry. I knew what I needed, but I couldn't take it without letting go of my tenuous control. So I took something else instead.

Carson was starting to buck, so, using my feet, I braced myself above him with my knees bent. Carson grabbed my hips, jackhammering up into me, while I continued to rub my swollen clit. He started to come, hard. I could feel it spurting inside me, filling me up and dripping everywhere. It was wet and dirty and fucking delectable. I lost myself to the bliss, pretending it was anyone but Carson beneath me. Pretending I was a free woman who could do as she pleased. He kept going until I was following him into ecstasy the next moment. My orgasm ripped through me like fire, fast, rough and hot. Just the way I needed it from him right now. There was no love or affection between us, just two bodies fucking for our own selfish pleasure.

Coming down from my high after a few moments, I rolled off of Carson, who was breathing heavily. There was cum all over me, and I suddenly felt disgusting. Now that my head had cleared, I wanted it off me. His dazed eyes were glossy, and his expression appeared sated. Almost immediately, I wanted him to leave. I should have felt horrible for using him like this. I should have felt like a bitch, like the world's worst girlfriend. And maybe I was, but I was past the point of caring. Besides, he didn't deserve it. He didn't deserve me or my pussy or my heart or my hand in marriage he still thought was his.

"Fuck, baby doll," he breathed, raking a hand through his messy blond hair.

I bit my tongue, seriously wondering if he realized how much that name pissed me off. He'd called me baby doll since the day we met at fourteen years old, when he'd said I looked like a porcelain doll, and the name sort of stuck. At the time, back when my life wasn't so screwed up and I saw him as just a handsome boy with cute dimples and pretty eyes, I was flattered. Now, that name just reminded me of what I really was—breakable.

"Serenity?"

Oh, right. He was still here. "I'm kind of tired," I breathed out, swinging my legs over the side of the bed before quickly padding to my bathroom. Turning on the shower, I let steam fill the room, breathing in deeply as I let the water heat.

Hands snaked around my middle and Carson's chin landed on my shoulder, causing my whole body to lock up. "Want some company?" he asked softly.

"No thanks." I shrugged, trying to make the roll of my shoulders look unintentional, but neither of us were stupid or clueless.

"What's your problem?" He pulled back, spinning me so that I faced him head on. We were almost the same height.

"I told you, I'm tired." Rolling my eyes wasn't exactly smart, but I couldn't help it. I was tired...and lightheaded, my body crying out for sustenance I refused to give it. I'd never get used to this empty feeling, and I'd probably just keep seeking out ways to fulfill that need.

"Bullshit," he sneered, eyes raking over me skeptically.

"Fuck off, Carson."

"So it's like that then?" A bitter twist to his lips had my hackles rising. "Fuck me and then fuck off, right? Just like always." He huffed out a bitter laugh. "You know, maybe your dad has the right idea, smacking you around sometimes—"

My hand cracked over his cheek before I could stop myself. "Get out."

It wasn't the first time he'd said something like that in the heat of the moment and it wouldn't be the last, but I was getting tired of hearing it. Carson was one of those men who believed a woman's place was in the home while men ran the world. He was like Ryan Harker in that way. It was why he'd eventually follow in his own asshole father's footsteps, and I knew he expected me to tag along and play the good little wife someday. Little did he know that was absolutely not happening.

His hand twisted in my hair as I turned away, not in the good way either. Hot breath wafted over my face as my neck was wrenched backwards. "Or what, *baby doll*?" His voice was deadly calm. I hated when he did that. It was worse than yelling. When he got quiet, I knew he was pissed.

"Carson, stop," I gritted out through clenched teeth. My heart was hammering painfully as I held the monster at bay. She didn't like the way his fingers felt in her hair. "I'm sorry if I'm being a bitch, I just don't feel well. I promise, that's all it is."

I hated begging. Hated placating his fragile ego and pretending to be weaker than I knew I was. But the way his fingers fisted my long hair, tugging at my scalp, was a stark reminder of what he was capable of. I wasn't by any means a fighter. I had a mouth on me and I was pretty sure I could handle myself if it was life or death, but fighting with my fists wasn't my strong suit. Sheltered daughters of politicians had no use for fighting, and my mother would've had an aneurysm if she saw me in anything less than heels and pearls. The more I denied my true nature and denied my body what it needed to grow strong, the more defenseless I became, against Carson and my father both.

"Watch your fucking tone next time, Serenity. You're a good fuck, but it's not going to protect you forever." The tips of his fingers ran down my arm. Nose pressed into my flesh, he inhaled deeply, making my mouth flood with saliva. "Someday, this pretty face will change, you know. Someday, I won't have an excuse to make sure it stays pretty."

Those words rattled around in my brain and settled in my gut like poison. *Someday, this pretty face will change.* It would, he was right, but it didn't have to. I could stay this age forever if I gave myself over to the monster. I could do it. I could wait for my father and Carson to age and wither and die. It would be so easy to bite down into his tender jugular. The taste alone would be...

Releasing my hair, Carson shoved me forward, but I caught myself on the half wall next to the shower. The room was thick with steam now, and it was stifling. Sweat beaded on my naked flesh. I could smell him on me, could feel him everywhere. His cum still dripped down my thighs, and I needed it gone. I needed to be clean.

"Don't forget," he said as he made his way towards the door, straightening his tie back into place, "I'm picking you up after your classes on Friday. We have dinner planned with some colleagues at seven. I'll send a dress over tomorrow morning. Wear your hair down."

I gritted my teeth, biting my tongue against the *fuck no* I wanted to hurl at him. Carson loved to dictate what I wore and how I looked, especially in front of those he deemed important—his *colleagues.* People who thought they ran Noc City. He wanted to show me off like a trophy. Sometimes, I cursed my looks. Sometimes, I hated myself for it.

I gave him a curt nod, not bothering to respond verbally. For a moment, he gave me a look like he might berate me for the disrespect, but a moment later, his phone rang. Literally saved by the bell. With one last lingering sweep of my body that made me feel oily all over, Carson left the room, the door clicking shut loudly.

A sob ripped from my lips the moment he was gone, and I practically flung myself into the shower. I didn't bother with my hair or washing my body right away. I couldn't stop crying. I hadn't had a good cry in days, and it seemed like all of it was ready to flood out at once. Looking down, red leaked over my fingers, traveling down my pale skin and swirling around the drain. My tears ran red these days, ever since that day twelve months ago when the monster woke up. I cried blood, and it only made me cry harder.

I sat in the center of the shower for forty-five minutes, not even caring that the water had run cold long ago. It didn't matter. I could barely feel it. I needed to purge these feelings right now. I needed to get them all out where nobody could see my shame, because when I faced the world again, my mask wouldn't slip. I'd do it. I'd do it for her.

CHAPTER 2
SERENITY

*A*t breakfast the next morning, my mother was silent. She barely looked up when I made my way into the kitchen. Her breakfast of toast and eggs was cold on her untouched plate, but she was vigorously slurping down a mug of black coffee. Somehow, I knew it wasn't just coffee.

I came to an abrupt halt at the sight of a man I didn't recognize. He stood back from the table towards the windows, hands clasped in front of him. He wore a sharp black suit, black tie, and had an earpiece in one ear. It was the standard guard uniform, but his face was unfamiliar. I knew every member of my father's security detail, but not this one.

"New goon?" I directed the question at my mother.

Her eyes briefly flickered up. Or...I assumed they did, given the upward tilt of her head. She was wearing a giant pair of dark sunglasses, probably nursing a massive hangover. "Sit down, Serenity."

I snorted, ignoring the sharp order in her tone. "Doesn't it ever get old, Mother?" She looked up, blonde brow arched, as I said, "Hearing your own voice buzzing around the room like an annoying little fly?"

Fuck, I really was a bitch. There was a time I'd never have dreamed of testing her this way, but things changed. She changed. I changed. She'd showed her true colors when it was most important, and now it was time to reveal mine.

She ignored the jab, used to my underhanded insults by now. She simply didn't care. "Ryan has hired you a new security detail. This is...Merrick?" It was a question, one directed at the hulking man by the kitchen bay windows. He nodded. "This is Merrick."

Ryan, she'd said before. Ryan Harker. Not *Dad*. Guess we were done pretending finally.

Spinning around, forgetting about the coffee I'd been about to pour, I placed my hands on my hips, eyes bouncing between her and *Merrick*. They stayed on Merrick. I'd passed him over in my quest for a cup of sweet, sweet morning nectar, but now I couldn't look away.

He was six foot three at least, with long bronze hair tied in a bun behind his head, grass green eyes, and a tanned face dotted with freckles. Deep shadows hung beneath his eyes, but they only made him more interesting to look at. He had a well groomed beard that matched the hue of his hair, and beneath the neckline of his suit collar, I could see a tattoo creeping up the side of his neck. He was a handsome bastard and better looking than most of my family's goons.

He stared at me, making eye contact and catching me off guard. Usually, our hired help avoided eye contact, especially the security detail. They didn't give a shit about us, not really. They protected us because it was what they were paid to do, but they didn't care about the day to day. They didn't care about protecting an abomination.

This guy, though... Merrick's eyes swept me from head to

toe, as if he has any right to make a judgement about me. As if his opinion mattered. I was acutely aware that I still wore nothing but a pair of Spandex shorts and an oversized shirt that nearly covered them. I tore my eyes away from the obscenely attractive bodyguard and looked back to find my mother once again absorbed in her spiked coffee. She looked miserable.

"What happened to the old ones?" I asked in a bored tone.

"None of your concern, Serenity."

"Were they at least vetted?" She was getting on my last fucking nerve.

"Of course they were—"

"Would you like to see my credentials?" came a deep, male voice from the other side of the room. Merrick. He was Irish, that thick accent was a dead giveaway. It lilted off his tongue like rich honey.

I whipped my head in his direction, raising a brow. "Excuse me?"

His face was stony. Not a hint of an emotion. Our eyes held, and in his I could see danger, a cold, simmering danger. This man held a certain rage inside of him, but he was very good at keeping it inside. He didn't respond, but I hadn't expected him to. We both knew I'd heard what he said.

"We don't pay you to be a smart ass," I snapped, turning around to pour some coffee. I refused to let that heavy stare get to me.

"Please don't make a fuss," said my mother. "We have enough to worry about right now. Just let them do their jobs without complaining for once. Can you do that?"

I wanted to lash out. She spoke to me sometimes like I was a child and not a twenty-four-year-old woman who had

endured far too much for my age. But this one time, I didn't
have it in me to argue. Despite the fact that this man's
knowing eyes made me itch, I knew he was needed. He
looked capable, I supposed. I just hoped that danger in his
eyes would translate to protection. I shivered, remembering
the last time my bodyguards had failed at their jobs. My
brother was six feet underground because of it.

I took a deep pull of my coffee, tasting nothing. It
warmed my belly though as I turned around and leaned
against the countertop. Tilting my head from side to side, I
felt my neck pop in a satisfying way that had me sighing. A
throat cleared in the room.

Popping my eyes back open, I met Merrick's hard stare.
A fire burned there. There was something about the way he
was watching me that had my whole body feeling flushed. I
couldn't let him know, though. I needed to keep my
wayward hormonal feelings to myself. There was no way I
was about to throw myself at a hired goon. Nope. My
monster would have to get her rocks off elsewhere.

"I have class most of the day and then a fitting later.
Carson's got some big dinner at his place tomorrow, so don't
expect me anywhere."

My mother just hummed in response. I knew she didn't
actually give a shit. Tossing the rest of my coffee in the sink,
I abandoned the kitchen and my drunk parent, making my
way back through the house. It wasn't until I reached the
staircase that I realized there were eyes on me. I whipped
around, coming face to face with Merrick. He'd followed me
from the kitchen, close on my heels.

"What are you doing?" Folding my arms over my chest, I
eyed the man with disdain.

"Following you." So matter of fact. Unapologetic.

"Not in my own home, you're not."

"Looks like I am, lass." He shifted on his feet, squaring his shoulders. It looked like he was trying to contain a smirk.

Hands on my hips, I had to crane my head to see into his green eyes as I walked closer. And boy, were they green, though slightly yellow towards the middle, like a sunflower in a grass field. I shook off the imagery, pretty sure I was starting to lose my mind.

"I don't know if this is your first time around the block, but you only need to follow me once we leave this property. I don't need a babysitter."

"Babysitter?" he asked, arching a bronze brow. "Do babysitters usually throw themselves in front of bullets for you?"

"You talk too much already. I'll let you know when I leave the house, but until then, leave me alone."

Merrick's face remained bland. Bored. "Just doing my job. If you interfere with that job, I'll have to report it to Mr. Harker."

My blood ran cold as I stepped closer to the Irish behemoth. I knew I wasn't frightening or intimidating in any way, but there was venom in my stare at least. "I dare you."

Those green eyes darkened. Jade was the new color, and I found that I liked it on him. "Oh, I like a challenge, little lady." That brogue made the hairs on my arms stand. I could feel the heat of his body so close to mine, and I knew if I was smart, I'd back away. "I really do," he said, lowering his voice to a near whisper. I didn't know where he got the balls to behave this way with one of the most important families in the state, but he'd learn sooner or later.

I backed up, tired of wasting my time on this stranger. He was a goon, nothing more. A hotheaded babysitter who didn't know his place yet. "Stay out of my way, okay? Seriously, I'm not someone you want to make an enemy of." My threats were empty, but he didn't know that. I started to turn around, ready to get this shitty ass day started.

"Off to your chambers then, princess. I'll be here when you need an escort." Sensual lips beneath that scruff curled up on the sides as he winked, but his eyes remained cold. I couldn't tell if he actually found amusement in taunting me, or if he was forcing it. It was hard to get a read on this guy.

I turned from him, not bothering with a retort, knowing it wouldn't go anywhere. I needed to get ready for classes, and Trix would be calling any second now, wondering where I was. My cousin was impatient and liked to get to campus at least an hour before class. We had a cute little coffee shop not far from my civics class with a nice view of the mountains that surrounded the walls of Noc City.

I felt Merrick's stare all the way up the curving staircase. Without looking over my shoulder, I knew he was just standing there, waiting for me to disappear. He thought he was unnerving me. He was, but I wouldn't show it. I'd dealt with cocky goons before. They all came out of security training thinking they were going to be some sort of Rambo type, when really, they were nothing but glorified babysitters. Not many had lasted, and my last ones were seasoned enough to know their place. I could already tell I was going to have my work cut out for me with this guy following me around all day.

I dressed for the day in a sensible dark red sweater dress, black tights, and heeled boots. I left my hair loose, knowing the bruising on the back of my neck had yet to fully fade. My father slipped up two nights ago, again. He'd been doing that a lot lately. Usually, the bruises were discrete, in places that a camera couldn't capture by accident. The scars etched across my back were reminders of how much that man hated me. If I'd given into my cravings, the marks would've been fully healed by now, but alas, I was as weak as a human.

I tried to leave through the side entrance. I told our driver, Gregory, that I'd be leaving at eight o'clock sharp, so I knew he'd be waiting for me. I was hoping to avoid Merrick. He probably didn't know the layout of our property yet, so he wouldn't expect me to sneak out this direction. Satisfied with myself, I grinned when I saw Gregory already standing next to the open door of our family's limousine. He smiled back at me, a grandfatherly smile that he'd given me since I was born.

"Good morning, Miss Harker. Fall is in the air at last." He breathed in deeply as leaves floated around us, turning orange, red, and yellow in the crisp air. Fall *was* on the way, I realized. September first. The air was crisp, and the smell of dead leaves heralding the winter to come had me sucking in lungfuls. The summer had been a long one, and we were all eager to put the oppressive heat behind us.

"Morning, Greg. How's Kathy?" I asked as I approached.

His brown eyes lit up. "She won another tournament over the weekend. Can't seem to shut her up about it either."

His wife was a sweet woman. Kathy was on the senior golf team down at the country club, and Gregory loved to brag about her skills. She was a witch and always made me charms for the holidays. I loved the way his jovial eyes lit up. It made my heart squeeze sometimes. What I wouldn't give for a future like that, with a love that transcended age, wealth, status, and rules.

I slid into the seat and let darkness envelop me. Ever since the attack twelve months ago, the windows had been tinted nearly black and bulletproofed. The door closed, and silence fell. The overhead light was on, casting the interior in a dull glow. I immediately knew I wasn't alone. Two men sat across from me, and about six feet separated us. It didn't surprise me to see Merrick here. Apparently, I hadn't given him nearly enough credit.

"Morning, lass." His deep brogue rolled through the silent limo. I didn't respond, just sat there and stared at the two men, trying to convey that they hadn't rattled me. Merrick chuckled. "I don't believe you've had the pleasure of meeting my colleague." He gestured to the other goon.

I nearly snorted at the word *colleague*. They were mall cops. Grunts. The other man was still and silent, watching me closely, and our eyes met and held. This guy was handsome too. Too handsome. I squinted at him, instantly suspicious. He had dark blond hair, cut short, parted sideways, and shaved short on the sides. Clean shaven and square jawed, he had what looked like a barbell piercing in his right eyebrow that framed chocolate brown eyes—eyes that were narrowed right back at me, as if he were sizing me up.

I gave them a curling, bitter smile that wasn't exactly friendly. "So, which one of you lost the bet that got you stuck here with me?" It had to have been one of them. I couldn't imagine they'd volunteered for this shit. Not after what happened. Neither of them laughed.

"This is Faust," Merrick continued, introducing his comrade. "Your father requested us specifically for your protection—"

"Ryan Harker is *not* my father, so jot that down right now." The biting words slipped out before I could shut myself up, but it wasn't like they didn't know already... Or did they? I wasn't sure what my father had decided to tell them. Merrick and Faust didn't react, just waited for my outburst to be over. They probably assumed I was being a brat. Oh well, if it got them to shut the fuck up for a while, I didn't care.

"As I was saying... We're here for your protection. Only yours. We have your school itinerary, the names and descriptions of your friends and acquaintances, as well as a direct line to your...boyfriend." He said *boyfriend* with a raised brow and a bitter smirk that I didn't appreciate.

"Would you like my social security number and my first born too?"

"We have your social, sweetheart," said Faust. It was the first he'd spoken. His accent was Northern American, clipped and to the point. I couldn't get a read on him either. He was stone faced, and his brown eyes were cold.

"Naturally," I said dryly.

We lapsed into a tense silence as the limousine moved through town. I tried to pretend I couldn't feel their eyes on me watching every single twitch, every breath, and every subtle shift. It was unnerving, but I pretended it didn't faze me.

The college was on the other side of Noc City, closer to the downtown portion that held the capitol building, the museum we'd visited yesterday for the press conference, and the courthouses. Noc was huge with respect to the surrounding woodland area. Not as large as New York City, but pretty close. It was progressive, I supposed. Humans and darklings coexisted for the most part, but outside the city was still a huge question mark.

Darklings had come out of hiding seventy years before I was born. Vamps, werewolves, witches and everything in between. What was once the source of human tall tales and legends, was now a part of everyday society. They'd fought for their rights the whole seventy plus years, and humans, for the most part, were accepting of them. The Coexist

Doctrine signed by the heads of every race declared sanctuary cities around the world as neutral zones. Noc City was one of those sanctuary cities.

There was one college in all of Noc City, and I attended it, if only to make my father look good. He thought if I mingled with the masses and pretended to sympathize with them, he'd appear more benevolent. I would've fought it, like I did with most things, if it weren't for the fact that going to class was my time to escape for a little while.

It was still early, and my stomach grumbled. I needed coffee and food, asap. Trix was blowing up my phone, so I stashed it in my coat pocket. Sometimes, that girl was a bit much. She was the closest to me in age out of all the cousins, and we'd been close since infancy. Trix was a handful on the best of days, but I loved her regardless. She was also sort of the black sheep of the family. After turning eighteen, she hightailed her ass out of her parent's house and moved to the college campus. She was now an avid darkling rights protester and activist, much to the embarrassment of our political family.

Sometimes, I envied Trix that sort of freedom. If there was a way I could get my mother out from under Ryan Harker's thumb, I'd be right there alongside Trix. I hated the nasty rhetoric he tried to spread through the city and its gullible people. The influence he had over the humans was terrifying. Noc City was progressive, but it seemed like my father was dead set on turning back the clock. I didn't understand his hatred for the darklings. I mean, I guessed I could understand if the sudden dislike sprouted up the day my mother was forced to admit she had a torrid affair with a vampire, but that wasn't the case. Ryan Harker had it out for the darklings since before I was even in the picture, and had worked his way up in office so that one day, he'd hold enough sway over the general public.

The facts were this—humans still outnumbered the darklings ten to one, and despite having supernatural abilities, they still didn't have the upper hand. Entire factions of bigoted humans had formed hate groups, making it their sole purpose in life to exploit the darkling's weaknesses. It was disgusting, and unfortunately for me, I was associated with that rhetoric as Ryan Harker's cherub faced daughter, the sweet young woman who did as her daddy told her. I couldn't escape it.

We pulled up to campus near the atrium. Already, I spotted Trix barreling out of the glass double doors and heading for the limo. Sometimes, I wondered if she had a tracker on me. Again, I didn't wait for Gregory to let me out. I was perfectly capable of opening doors, and I needed to get out from under the heavy weight of my goon's stares.

Trix had her arms around my shoulders in the next second. "Christ, woman, what the hell took you so long? We barely have time to grab a latte!" Her black waves bounced along her shoulders. Trix was wearing one of her home-made screen printed T-shirts that read *#darklingrights*, and subsequently, she was drawing in a few pointed stares.

"We have thirty minutes! Chill." I extracted her from my body. "I'm freaking starving."

Her attention drifted over my shoulder as a metaphorical shadow loomed. I knew my new babysitters were standing behind me from the way her green eyes scanned them from head to toe appreciatively.

"Uh, babe, is there something you need to tell me?" Hands on her hips, Trix squinted at me.

"Trix, meet grumpy and grumpier." I gestured to the two

lugheads. "They'll be stalking me for the foreseeable future."

A grin twisted her cherry red lips as she shook her head. "Sometimes, I envy you, cousin."

I laughed, but it was strained. She had no idea how badly I envied her. She didn't know all the details. She didn't know what happened behind closed doors. She didn't know I wasn't a human and that the revelation rocked my life off course forever. I'd been building up to telling her the truth, but for some reason, I couldn't bring myself to do it. Trix was the one constant in my life that was always reliable, and the thought of her suddenly looking at me differently made my stomach clench with uncertainty.

"C'mon, let's get those coffees. Seriously, we're barely gonna make it across campus as it is." Turning us both towards the little corner café, she cast a wink over her shoulder at the guys. "Hope you're up for a sprint, boys."

Still, they made no effort to respond, just followed behind us silently. I dared a glance over my shoulder and saw Faust sweeping his eyes over the surrounding area, jaw tight and barely breathing. He looked tired in all honesty. Like Merrick, Faust seemed to have purple shadows beneath his eyes, making me wonder if the men ever got any sleep. I must've been staring for too long, because our eyes met and held for a heartbeat. I was the first one to look away, while he just stared back blankly. Snapping out of it, I ignored the uneasy flip to my stomach and let Trix lead me away.

We got our drinks, and I choked down a muffin. It took me all of two minutes on our walk to class to chug the hot bean water, as Trix liked to call it, while she nursed her chai tea. Civics flew by in a breeze, and then we were off to public speaking for another three. Soon, we were heading out into the afternoon heat. The crisp air Gregory had waxed on about was long gone, and I could feel beads of sweat building on my neck. I used to love the summer heat and the long days, but in the last few months, I found myself craving fall and winter more and more. I didn't like to think about why that was.

The college campus was packed today with humans. All humans during the daylight. Though the vampires were the only race unable to brave the sunlight, I supposed the rest of the darklings decided to live in the night in solidarity. It became somewhat of an unspoken rule, the segregation of the species. Even in this progressive city where we were all supposed to live in harmony, there was a divide that everyone seemed reluctant to cross.

Every once in a while, a brave witch or werewolf would wander into the light, taking a human studies class or even a seminar or two, but it was frowned upon. I never saw what the big deal was. The whole point of sanctuaries like Noc City was to integrate the humans and the darklings. After seventy years, you'd think the prejudice would have stopped, but humans were persistent in their quest to be the top of the food chain. Whether it be weapons or sheer numbers, they always seemed to be at the top.

It still felt strange, referring to humans as a group I was no longer a part of. Up until the tragedy twelve months ago, I *was* one of them. I'd been ignorant, self-assured, and small. I'd never stopped to think about what life was like for the darklings and how my father's beliefs challenged their right to have normal lives in a city that was meant to shelter them. How Ryan Harker rose to power spewing his hatred and disgusting doctrine was a mystery I still couldn't puzzle out. It wasn't like I was wholly blind to it though. I was just powerless under his thumb, so I chose to pretend like it didn't exist. Shameful, I know.

"We're going out tonight," Trix said as we waited for Gregory to come pick us up. She was tapping on her phone, not looking at me, confident I'd just go along with it as usual.

"Cool, have fun. Don't do anything I wouldn't do." I really didn't feel like going out, not tonight. Not when I just wanted to go home and mentally psych myself up to spending the next evening with Carson and his friends.

"*We*, as in you and me, Ren. You're going, and I don't care what you have to tell Elodie. Tell her you've got study group or you're fucking Carson. Frankly, I don't even care. You're twenty-four going on eighty, so you're coming to Rue tonight."

I could feel Merrick's gaze boring a hole into the side of my head. It was hard to keep my cheeks from flaming. I didn't need to give that man any more ammunition against me. Yeah, okay...I was boring as shit these days, but there was a reason for that, even if I hadn't come clean to my cousin.

Rue. Trix loved that place. I'd only been there once with her and her activist friends. Rue was a vamp club downtown, and it was dark, sexy, and really hard to get in to.

"We'll be waiting in line for hours," I mumbled, none too impressed.

Trix rolled her eyes. "Do you have any idea who you are?"

"Uh..."

Placing her hands on my shoulders, Trix looked me square in the eyes, as if it made her argument any more enticing. "Having the senator's daughter show up to their club would look great for the vamps. They'll probably give us a VIP table and free drinks."

"So you want me for my status, then." I folded my arms,

trying to keep a grin at bay. I knew my cousin wasn't actually that shallow.

Her eyes narrowed. "You're going."

"Fine," I groaned. It was pointless to argue. "But we're getting ready at your place. My dad won't get back from Chicago until tomorrow, and I don't think I can deal with my mom any more today."

Trix wore a smug smile as we watched Gregory pull the limo to a stop. "I thought you'd see things my way. Just go with it, Ren. You need to cut loose. I saw you on TV yesterday. You looked like someone shoved a pole up your ass."

I snorted. "Bitch."

"Loser."

"Radical."

"Princess."

My hand flew to my chest, aghast. "Okay, ouch."

She just laughed, turning away and throwing her arms around Gregory's shoulders. "Hey, old Greg!"

"Hello to you too, Miss Castwell." He patted her on the back, shaking his head. "Where to?"

"To my place," she declared, already sliding into the limo. "We're going out tonight, so we need you on standby."

I gave Gregory an apologetic smile and a shrug, and said, "The girl gets what she wants."

He just chuckled, eyes sliding to the two bodyguards behind me. He nodded to them curtly. "In you go, Miss Harker."

I was about to slide in after Trix when I felt a hand on the small of my back. My entire body turned to stone at the unexpected touch, and a bruise just below my ribs gave a sharp pulse of pain. I'd almost forgotten it was there, courtesy of my father's heavy foot. I was too slow to school my reaction and stop the flinch, so I whipped my head over my shoulder, only to see Faust right behind me, ushering me into the back of the car. Our eyes connected, and his seemed to darken as they flickered to where his palm now skimmed my back. Twin pools of tilled earth, shadowed by purple hued bags that somehow just served to make him more handsome, looked confused at my reaction.

That palm burned through to my skin, but it was a cold burn. I could feel it through the thick fabric of my sweater dress. Cold...too cold. I frowned down at the touch, but he pulled away in a heartbeat, staring me down as if daring me to say something. With a sneer, I tore my eyes from his and followed my cousin into the car, making sure to slide all the way to the other side, avoiding my goons the entire way to Trix's place.

CHAPTER 3
SERENITY

The campus was large enough that student housing was a little less than a mile away. Grouped together in a cluster of brick buildings, the dorms were unisex and on the nicer side for a college.

Trix had a suite all to herself, after her roommate transferred out last semester unexpectedly. They hadn't assigned her anyone else in the short time since she'd been gone, so one of the rooms was used to store my cousin's clothes and makeup. She had a nice living room with a kitchenette, which wasn't much more than a sink, microwave, and mini fridge, but it was better than what most dorms boasted.

I sent Merrick and Faust to the living room to wait, since they insisted on following us all the way up to the suite. Apparently, they were serious about watching me closely. As much as it aggravated and unnerved me, I couldn't help but feel a little bit safer knowing I had eyes looking out for things I was oblivious to. Twelve months wasn't nearly long enough to take away the itch of someone watching me. Someone...hunting me.

They'd missed last time, killing the wrong Harker instead. I couldn't afford to be caught unaware, so for now, I'd put up with the two broody men. Luckily, both of them were dressed just fine for clubbing, especially at a place like Rue. The dress code was pretty strict. Men had to wear suits, and women had to get just as dolled up. Or I guessed they could wear a suit if they preferred. At this point in the evening, I was heavily considering it myself.

Trix stuck me in a red dress so dark, it could've almost passed for black. The fabric was so thin, it felt like water cascading over my pale skin. It hit me mid thigh and the straps were incredibly thin, but the back wasn't as exposed as I thought it would be and my hair covered the rest. I'd been worried about letting those scars show, but the dress would do just fine.

I paired the dress with knee high lace up boots and straightened my long white blonde hair into a sleek, pearly curtain. Trix tried to get me to put it up to show off my neck, but I knew it would only raise questions, as my father's fingerprints were still visible there. Trix wore a royal blue minidress and a lace choker that played nicely against her pitch black hair, making her look like a gothic fairy princess. It took us barely a half hour to finish our makeup—bright red lips and winged black liner for me, matte black lipstick and sparkles around her greenish eyes for her. We didn't look related in the slightest, given the fact that we were, in fact, cousins on my mom's side. I got most of my looks from Elodie, but my eyes were my own. They were a dark chestnut brown, and I assumed they came from my biological father.

"So, when are we going to talk about the male models in my living room?" Trix asked cheekily, leaning against her vanity and crossing her arms over her chest while she waited for me to finish up.

"I don't know what you're talking about." I sniffed, fighting a smile.

"Bullshit, bitch. Your dad must have lost his damn mind."

I had the urge to correct her and tell her that Ryan Harker was not and would never be my father. There was an overwhelming urge to separate myself from him building up every single day. Now that I knew we shared no DNA, I needed to validate it. I fought the urge, not in any way ready for that life changing revelation.

"They're assholes, but they seem capable enough." I shrugged. "Not like the last ones…"

Flicking my eyes to hers, I watched her face soften. "What happened to them, anyway?"

A pit formed in my stomach, remembering the days that came after. "I try not to think about it. Never heard from them again. You can probably thank Ry—my dad for that."

I shuddered to think about what happened to my old bodyguards. They were both on the older side, pushing fifty, and only a few years away from retirement. I'd liked them for the most part. I was used to their ever looming shadows, and they'd always kept me safe. But that day…when the bombs went off and those bullets changed everything…

"All right," Trix said with a clap of her hands, snapping me out of dark memories. "Let's do this shit. Bryan and Cade are already at Rue, but they can't get in without you."

I snorted. "I'm really starting to think I'm being used here."

"Shut up." She waved me away.

We found the guys in the living room, standing around awkwardly. I guessed I should've felt kind of bad for them, but I really didn't. This was what they signed up for. I was suddenly more aware than ever of my exposed skin, though. I met Merrick's eyes first as they swept me from head to toe. I expected to see lust there, the way every male I'd ever met in my life usually reacted to me, but there was nothing except icy detachment. I didn't know if it was forced or not, but it made my stomach tighten uneasily.

Faust made his way to the door without looking at me and opened it for us all to file out. When I went to pass him, I was jerked back by a strong hand on my arm, forcing me to halt. I looked up, ready to rip into him for touching me like he had any right to, but the look in those dark eyes had my mouth drying up quickly.

"Do you think it's wise to parade yourself around the vampires, Serenity?" He spoke quiet enough that Trix couldn't hear. She was already halfway up the hallway, but Merrick was hanging back.

"I'm not a child. I can go out and enjoy myself if I want to."

"It's reckless and selfish," he muttered, hand tightening on my bicep. "You're putting your cousin at risk."

My eyes narrowed on the fingers gripping my skin, mind going blank. Suddenly, I could see the bruising, feel the licks of heat and pain and throbbing. He let go of my arm abruptly, causing me to wobble, but he steadied me with a hand on my hip. That touch once again burned through me with a cold that was so intense, I almost flinched away. The way he was looking at me had me wondering what was going on here exactly. I watched the way his eyes fought against the urge to flicker down and his fingers flexed.

"It's your first day on the job, so I'll give you a pass. But if you think you have any right to tell me how to live my life, then I won't hesitate to put in for your transfer. There are plenty of henchmen more than willing to take your place." I was lying. He knew it, too.

Those dark eyes flashed, and he moved in closer. "Trust me, it wasn't hard to land the job," he spat out. "You're going to have to get used to someone telling you what to do. I'm not going anywhere and neither is Merrick. You're stuck with us. We all know what happened last time daddy let go of the leash." Each word was a blade piercing my chest. I had to stand there and pretend I wasn't dying inside. "How many more people have to die for you, Serenity?"

For a moment, it was like stepping back in time. I could remember the sounds and the smells of gunfire and bombs. There was blood in my mouth and fire racing over my skin. After Sean had died, I had a couple weeks where I went a little off the rails and endangered his security. I didn't care that terrorists were still loose in the city, all I cared about was numbing the pain.

My eyes flickered between his, and I detected not a single ounce of remorse. He meant every word. I was a liability. It was my fault Sean was dead. He was only trying to protect me in his last moments. It was my fault for being what I was. Faust didn't know it yet, but I was even more of an outsider than he could ever imagine. A half-blood. An unwanted child of the night that never should have existed. Neither human nor vampire. Nothing. But to Faust and probably Merrick too, I was an annoying, rich brat who needed to be leashed. He didn't know a thing about me, save for what the public assumed.

"Your cousin is probably halfway down the street, lass. We need to get going." Merrick's voice broke through the tense stare off.

Backing up a step, I hadn't realized how close Faust and I were. But he was too tall for me to have any hope of intimidating him with my proximity. If anything, it probably just looked comical. I reached past him, making sure to avoid brushing my body against him, and shut Trix's door. It locked automatically. Without another look at the hotheaded man in front of me, I quickly turned and made my way down the hallway.

Rue was overflowing with partygoers dressed to the nines. The line alone stretched down the street and around the corner of the building. We were in the heart of Nocturne District.

The entire ten block radius was owned by the Nocturne Vampire Coven, and they enjoyed their opulence. It was a stark difference between the human portion of the city, which tended to be more commercial looking and bland. Nocturne was the opposite. Most of the buildings were fashioned out of brick and stone, reminiscent of gothic architecture, cathedrals, and old French style buildings. The streets were cobblestone, and cars were relegated to a strict ten mile per hour speed limit. It was a slower way of life in Nocturne, the people there in no hurry. Why would they, with eternity stretched out before them?

There were terraces overlooking the streets filled with people drinking from long stemmed glasses. Wrought iron lamp posts dotted every street corner and beautiful, otherworldly vampires gathered at every turn. Blood red eyes watched the limo as we pulled up to the entrance of Noc City's most infamous club. I didn't even bother asking Gregory to pull up near the back of the line, because Trix was absolutely right—they'd let me in without blinking.

I'd probably catch hell for being here tonight. The

moment Ryan saw the first headline about my presence at the vamp club, he'd descend into a fit of rage. I was just thankful he was in Chicago and not at home with my mother, who would likely serve as an outlet for that rage.

I stashed my handbag beneath the seat of the limo. I didn't trust anyone in Nocturne and needed to have both hands free. Trix was topping off her lip gloss, waiting as Gregory came around and opened the door for us. I could see people at the entrance of the club. Some of them hopeful humans, but most of them were vampires and witches. They were trying to peer into the darkly tinted windows, trying to see who was important enough to warrant such an entrance.

"This is your last chance, princess. Turn around now and go home like a good girl," said Faust. His low voice threatened to make me shiver, but I reigned it in. I didn't bother acknowledging him and had done a pretty good job at pretending he wasn't there the entire car ride, no matter how strange it felt to have those eyes pinning me to the seat.

I didn't give a shit if he thought this was a bad idea. I needed one night to feel normal. To pretend life wasn't just one blunder after the other. For tonight, I was free of my father. Free of Carson. Free of the walls of my father's fortress that stifled my will to keep on living. For the first time today, I couldn't feel the bruises under my dress.

Trix got out ahead of me, and the flash of hundreds of cameras erupted. I followed out after her, at this point in my life, completely unfazed. I knew my camera angles, knew how to smile with just enough cheek to make the tabloids bust a metaphorical nut, knew how to work them and make them crave more. Tonight, I felt like fucking with Faust a little, so I spun a few times, letting the paparazzi eat it up.

Loud murmurs filled the night air as I stepped past the

camera flashes. Trix looped her arm with mine as we made our way towards the entrance, where two burly bouncers stood in front of red velvet ropes. They were already speaking into their earpieces, likely warning the staff inside that the senator's daughter was here. I hated to sound so self important, but Trix was once again right. It looked good on the vamps to allow me in here. With all the nasty shit my father said about them, it was somewhat of a show of rebellion and solidarity on my part. A show I didn't normally go out of my way to display, but perhaps after tonight, I'd try a bit harder.

Women glared at us as we passed, arms crossed petulantly over their busty chests and makeup covered eyes looking us up and down as if they didn't understand the hype. They were just jealous they had to wait in line like peasants. Little did they know I actually envied them. Little did they know I'd pay any price to switch places with them and live even a single day in their mundane shoes.

Trix waved at two men, who scooted their way through the crowd, shouldering people out of the way. One of them had long sandy hair and the other short milky chocolate hair. They were both lanky, but dressed immaculately. I recognized them as two of Trix's friends from her activism groups. Bryan and Cade, I assumed.

I felt Faust and Merrick behind us and knew they had their eyes scanning the crowd, on alert for any possible dangers. After the last attack, even I was feeling a bit antsy to get inside. I felt a hand on the small of my back again and stiffened, but it was just Merrick, who wasn't even looking at me when I looked up at him from over my shoulder. His jaw was tight, and the purple shadows under his eyes seemed more stark in the flashing lights. We made it past the bouncers, who just waved us on without much thought, and then we were thrust into immediate darkness with lights flashing every few seconds as strobes in the distance guided the way. The hallway was narrow, and the floor was made of some kind of black shining marble, making it seem as if we were walking on smooth black water.

Thumping music in the distance pulsed, and my heart sped up. Despite telling Trix I wasn't in the mood to go out tonight, I couldn't deny the excitement I now felt. I loved dancing and letting loose. Before everything in my life went down the drain, Trix and I frequented human clubs all the time, usually wearing wigs and caked on makeup to hide my identity, but tonight, I didn't care. Let them see me. That same feeling of giddiness I used to feel on those wild nights slithered through me right then.

We came to the end of the long hallway, and it was like a bubble of sound burst around us. The club was tinged in red, and dancing men and women in cages dangled from the high ceilings. On the walls were giant screens filled with exotic images of dancing, sex, lips, skin, and teeth. I could feel the beat of the trance music and immediately wanted to dance. But Trix had other ideas.

"Bar!" she shouted, tugging me along. She didn't really need to shout. I could hear her even if she whispered, but I couldn't let her know that. Her friends waved to us as they made their way to the dance floor.

I let her drag me over to a massive glass top bar that had red lights shining upwards, making the whole thing glow like undulating lava. Trix rattled off two drinks I'd never heard of, but as I looked around at the vampires sipping velvety red liquid that looked way too enticing, I prayed the bartender would come back with something normal. Normal, I could handle.

Two glasses slid over the bar top, and I went to throw

some money down, but the bartender shook her head. Her close cropped black hair made her look like a punk rocker, and her piercings glinted in the red lights. "No charge!" she said with a sleek smile, flashing two sparkling fangs. "Not for you, baby girl."

I should have seen it coming. She knew exactly who I was, and there was no way she was about to charge the famous Serenity Harker for a bland cocktail. I gave her a thank you smile, but when she turned around, I tossed the money in her tip jar, knocked my drink back in one gulp, and turned away before she could come back.

Merrick and Faust were standing behind me, glaring down at me with their arms crossed over their barrel chests. They looked both comically out of place with their earpieces and scowls, but still dressed to impress enough that nobody would bat an eye. I made a show of licking the drips of alcohol off my lips as I held Faust's gaze. To my satisfaction, his brown eyes briefly dipped to where my tongue slid over red lipstick, but in a heartbeat, he met my eyes again, unamused.

Merrick wore a wry smirk now, but his eyes were cold. I could tell he was at least somewhat amused with the way I fucked with Faust's short temper, but not enough to give me any sort of human emotion. In fact, I was pretty sure neither of them were even capable of the feat.

"If you sexy beasts don't mind," Trix interjected, suddenly coming up behind me and looping her arm over my shoulders, "I'm taking this one dancing!" She started to tug me away and Faust made a move to follow, but Trix cut him a warning glare. "It's just a dance, Cujo. You can watch from here."

At the sudden uncertainty in his eyes, I barked a laugh I had no willpower to contain . His mouth started to open, probably to tell my cousin off, but Merrick elbowed him. He gave Faust a pointed look, which he held for a too long moment, but I was done waiting around for their cryptic secret conversation.

A hand once again wrapped around my arm before I made it two steps, bringing both Trix and I to a grinding halt. I spun to face Merrick, who wore a scowl on his handsome face. "Stay where we can see you," he said sternly. "I mean it, Serenity. No wandering off."

I wrenched my arm out of his grasp without answering and spun away, fuming internally. I understood they were only trying to keep me safe, but for some reason, their particular brand of protection was grating on my very last nerve. I was determined not to let them ruin the night for me.

Trix led me onto one of Rue's three dance floors, and we wove into a writhing mass of bodies. All around us were vampires, witches, and humans, and maybe even a few wolves, which surprised me. Most of the time, the wolves weren't seen in places like this. They preferred to stick to pack lands just on the outskirts of the city and took lifelong mates, rather than dating and clubbing. But there were definitely a few of them here. I could smell them.

The witches were easy to spot. They had eyes that shone like magical jewels and usually wore jewelry adorned with all kinds of crystals, beads, tassels, and feathers. They were more of a free spirited race and loved to flaunt it.

I moved to the thumping beat and let it envelop me like a warm hug. Closing my eyes, I lost myself to it, shutting out the rest of the world. On the dance floor, people weren't staring at me, watching my every move and judging me. They were too absorbed in their own dance partners or the way the hypnotic trance flowed through their bloodstream.

The music was bewitched for sure. There was something magical about it that human clubs just couldn't seem to replicate. It made me wonder if this club employed witches as well as vamps.

Trix was dancing with a man off to my left. He was tall and burly, and his hands were all over my cousin like he didn't know where to touch first. Trix could handle herself and she was smiling, so I figured she didn't need me to intervene. Sweat dripped down my spine as I spun, arms up in the air, but a sudden chill snaked over my exposed skin, raising my arm hairs. I felt as if someone was watching me, and not just Merrick and Faust, who were no doubt perched on the floor above, watching my every move. No, this was someone else.

Opening my eyes, I locked gazes immediately with a man who stood on a raised platform at the end of the dance floor. He was incredibly tall, wearing a dark suit with no tie and a shining diamond watch on his wrist. Tattoos snaked up the sides of his neck, but they didn't detract from the refined aura he exuded.

I was still dancing, still feeling the music, but was unable to rip my gaze from his. His attention was honed on me, just me. I could feel the heat of it licking my skin and making my thighs burn. He was exactly my type. Carson was handsome, but I was growing tired of pretending I had any interest in being his girlfriend. He was a vile man, and I didn't think I could take much more of it. But this man...Perhaps he'd make a good rebound fuck for the night. Perhaps I needed to let loose for real and get Carson out of my system.

I was so lost in my thoughts that it took me a moment to realize the man was no longer standing on the platform. I looked around, desperately trying to locate him, but the lights were too dim and the club was packed with people.

My heart sank. I didn't want to look like an idiot and go chasing after some stranger. I wasn't that pathetic.

I was about to tell Trix I was heading back to the bar for another drink I couldn't actually feel, when hands snaked around my waist from behind. I stiffened, but a moment later, the musky scent of leather and smoke enveloped me, and when I looked down, I recognized that diamond watch. A slow smile curled my lips, and I started to move with the stranger. My ass was pressed against his hips as we swayed, and I could feel his hardness pressing into my back, making me shiver. Leaning back, I wrapped an arm around his neck, letting my head fall onto his chest. One of his palms skimmed my thigh, traveling higher until it grazed my abdomen. My thighs burned, begging me to rub them together. I felt achingly wanton tonight, needing desperately to forget myself for a while.

I turned in his arms and drew in a sharp breath as our eyes clashed up close. Red. His eyes were red, a deep crimson and black that filled the whites and made his olive skin even paler. A close cropped beard covered the bottom half of his face, making him look dashing and manly, and his midnight black hair was in a clean crew cut. He looked positively dangerous, as most vampires did. He grinned down at me, incisors glinting invitingly in the red lights.

Instead of feeling fear, like any normal human might, I felt the opposite—elation. I wasn't a human. I'd never been one to begin with, and my body called out to this vampire and made my veins sing for him. He was watching me, waiting for my reaction to his blood red eyes. He smiled when I did, and a gleam of something that looked like satisfaction filled his eyes.

I wound my arms over his shoulders, which were considerably higher up than I'd originally thought. He must have been well over six feet tall, just like my two bodyguards. I suddenly had a fleeting thought and wondered what they thought about my new dance partner, but I shook the it away a moment later. I shouldn't care what they thought. They were nothing more than attractive annoyances.

We danced with a sensual slowness, despite the fast beat of the music. It was like we were in our own little world, eyes locked as we held our bodies together. I could feel every hard ridge of him as I ground against him. His cock was growing harder against my stomach, and I wasn't even ashamed to admit I was grinding my pussy against his thigh as I straddled it. Zings of pleasure pulsed through me, and my clit grew sensitive. I could feel the roughness of his slacks, making my legs shake. I needed to come badly. I needed an outlet for this energy.

I was about to tell him we needed to get out of here, when there was a sudden burning in my gums, a familiar ache that sent dread curling in my gut. I stiffened, and so did the stranger. He cocked his head to the side, asking me with his eyes if everything was okay, but I just stumbled backwards, out of his arms. My gums felt like they were on fire, and I knew it was my fangs wanting to descend. I couldn't let it happen. There were too many humans around.

I mumbled a quick apology to my mystery man and fled the dance floor. Trix was too absorbed in her partner to pay attention, so I just kept going. I wove through bodies, and when I got to the edge of the dance floor, I took a dark hallway down a few narrow corridors, searching for a bathroom. Finding one that mercifully had no line out the door, I shoved my way in. It was a good thing vampires rarely needed to use the restroom, because it was empty. I stumbled to the sink and gripped the black marble hard enough that I thought I might crack it. Spitting into the sink a few times, I tried to rid my mouth of the saliva that filled it, begging me to take the sustenance I needed. I knew I needed blood. My body was craving it more and more with each day I denied myself.

My head was pounding, and the room seemed to spin. I knew that if I went back out to that club, there was a very real chance I might attack a defenseless human. Wouldn't that look amazing on the tabloids tomorrow...?

After a few moments, my mouth dried up and I no longer felt the ache in my gums. I squeezed my eyes shut, begging my heart to slow down, begging the monster to calm and retreat back into my subconscious. She didn't want to hide, didn't want to stay put. She wanted to rip and tear and devour. She craved it.

Opening my eyes, I gazed into the mirror, watching in horror as my red and black eyes slowly turned back to brown. When the vampire side of my anatomy took hold, the skin around my eyes tightened and small black veins snaked through the translucent color. I looked like a demon straight from a nightmare. The ice blonde hair and pretty face couldn't hide what lurked inside.

It took about twenty minutes for me to calm down. I was breathing in and out slowly, my mind blanking as the monster gave in and surrendered. Finally, I was feeling a little more in control, and my teeth felt normal. The air conditioning whirring overhead blew the sweaty strands of my hair back like a crisp breeze, and I raised my face up to bask in it. I stayed like that for another ten minutes, psyching myself up to rejoin the world. I swiped my fingers under my eyes, making sure my makeup was in place. Smoothing my hair with my fingers, I headed back out into the dark corridor, but I only made it two steps before I was yanked to the side.

I went to yelp, but a hand clamped over my mouth as someone dragged me through a door to my left. I struggled, but whoever had me was incredibly strong. Once through the door, I thought they would release me, but I was wrong. We suddenly moved faster than I'd ever moved before, my surroundings only a hazy blur as we careened down yet another long dark corridor, this one black as night rather than tinged with the red lights of the club. It took seconds for whoever it was to shove me into a room.

I turned around in a flash, immediately reaching for the closed door, when a gust of wind blew my hair back. I felt a presence at my back, a looming, all consuming presence. The smell of leather and smoke wafted around me, and suddenly, there was no question as to who'd trapped me in this room. It was my stranger, the beautiful man who only a half an hour ago, had his hands all over me. Turning around, I blinked at him. The room was dark, but my eyesight was advanced enough that I could see him despite the shadows. He was so tall, I had to crane my neck to meet his red eyes. They glowed with a feral intensity, and his shoulders were heaving as if he was trying to catch his breath.

"Who are you?" I asked, eyes flickering back and forth between his. They looked redder than they had in the club against the darkness of the room.

In a blink, he shoved me against the door, hard enough to knock the air out of me. My heart jumped to my throat as he held me there. His hands were immovable vices, and his smell consumed me. I couldn't figure out if I even wanted him to let me go. My head was muddied and confused, and I wasn't reacting to this situation the way I should have been. The way I would have twelve months earlier. My cravings were resurfacing, and the monster inside me craved sustenance. When it got this bad, I did things I knew were wrong, things I hoped I wouldn't regret later.

"I'm going to fuck you," he said plainly. His voice was deep and rumbly, making me shiver. He said the words so matter of fact, that my mind momentarily blanked.

"You—" I started to say, but he brought his body flush with mine, pressing his thigh between my legs.

"If you don't want this, say the word now and I'll let you leave. I never fuck a woman who doesn't want it, but I have a feeling you already made up your mind." He sounded so sure of what I wanted from him, and it scared me a little that he was right. "You have ten seconds to tell me no. After that, you're mine."

Fuck, he was serious. He really would fuck me against this door. A complete stranger. Did I want him to? The answer hit me instantly—I wanted him to fuck me. I wanted this stranger to ravage me and make me forget my own name. I suddenly wanted him to destroy me, to wipe every single trace of Carson from my memory. It was reckless. It was stupid and foolish to entertain the notion of succumbing to a vampire's charms. I knew I could very well be making a huge mistake, but I was beginning to realize I didn't care. I just didn't have it in me to care anymore.

I had no idea how much time had passed since he trapped me in here, but his grip grew heavier, and I noticed belatedly that I was grinding my hips, causing my pussy to rub on his thigh again. He brought his lips closer to mine, and I could feel cool breaths washing over my lips and the scratch of his beard on my skin.

"If we do this...I don't want to know you," I whispered against his mouth. "I don't want to know your name. I don't want to know anything about you, got it? I want you to fuck me, and then I want you to leave me alone." My words were cold and emotionless, surprising even myself, but I meant them. I had no interest in any kind of romantic relationship.

The red in his eyes flared, and his lips curled. "I think I can accommodate," he replied smoothly. Something like triumph was etched on his handsome face a moment before our lips finally clashed.

Hands cupped my ass, hoisting me up against the wall as his lips devoured mine. I ran my tongue along his lips, and he scraped his incisors along my tongue. I shivered. I'd never fucked a vampire before. The thought of it would have sent the old Serenity into a panic, but right now, all I could think of was the feel of his lips and teeth and strong, cold hands. All I wanted was the press of his cock against my clit. I hadn't worn any underwear tonight, and I was thanking every god in the heavens for that decision right now.

With a strength I never knew existed, the stranger lifted me up. As if I weighed no more than a feather, he literally lifted me up until I was practically sitting on his shoulders, back still leaning against the door. With his palms under my thighs, he kissed my bare flesh, and I relished the harsh scrape of his facial hair against me. There was no turning back now, and truth be told, I didn't want to. Call me a slut or a whore...it didn't matter. I was sick of living my life to the standards set out for me. I was tired of the only touch I received being at the hands of a sadist. I needed this.

Deciding to help him out, I pulled up my dress, exposing my bare pussy to his grinning face. Fuck, he was handsome. With his groomed black beard and tattoos peeking out from the collar of his expensive suit, I had a feeling this man was wealthy. He looked like the type who commanded people, a man people feared and respected.

I watched from above as his crimson eyes devoured me. I suddenly couldn't wait for his mouth to do the same, and he wasted no time after that. He balanced me there against the door as he brought his mouth to my pussy, swiping his tongue over my folds. I groaned, closing my eyes and tipping my head back as his tongue flattened, pressing on my clit and swiping in fast movements that had me catching my breath.

I ground against his face and wondered if he could even breathe as he ate me out. The feel of his beard against my core felt like heaven. He was incredibly strong, balancing me perfectly, never once wavering. My feet were resting on his shoulders now, and I could only imagine how utterly insane this position would have looked to a human. I let out a dark chuckle at the mental image.

He licked me faster now, and I felt heat building inside me. My clit pulsed, and I realized that anything I'd ever felt in bed with Carson was a blip on the radar compared to what this stranger was making me feel with just his mouth. We hadn't even fucked yet, and I was ready to come all over his face.

One hand left my ass, and somehow, the man kept me balanced without any effort. Fingers dipped into my pussy and, coupled with his tongue on my clit, I didn't stand a chance. A violent orgasm ripped through me, and I didn't even try to contain my scream. My thighs were shaking on the sides of his head, heat flushing through me as I gripped his hair tight enough it would have hurt a human man. His strokes slowed as I came down from the high, tongue lapping at my core leisurely, as if savoring the moment. I was breathing hard, panting, really. I slapped my hands to my forehead, wicking away the beads of sweat that had accumulated there. Soon, the man pulled away, carefully maneuvering me until I touched the ground.

"Holy shit," I breathed, holding a hand to my chest as my heart raged against it.

His palm came up on the side of my face, cupping my chin. For a split second, I almost had the urge to flinch. The realization settled like a rock in my gut. I was so used to Carson's mood swings that it was just reflex at this point. I let my gaze wander as I caught my breath. The room was still dark, but I was beginning to make out the details. There was a massive desk at the far wall, and every wall was covered in floor to ceiling bookshelves. Definitely not something I expected for a night club.

"Whose office is this?" I asked the man. "Should we find some—"

There was a commotion in the hallway that had my hackles rising. Shouts, bangs, and shuffling feet. The stranger noticed at the same time I did, and his open, friendly expression shuttered. "You need to get out of here," he snapped. Cold and detached again. "Go!" He backed away, eyeing the door behind me. When I hesitated, he urged me on again, shouting, "Go now!"

I didn't wait for more instruction before turning around and flinging the door open. I felt a rush of air at my back and turned to find the room completely empty—no sign of the vampire who'd once been there. There was an open window on the far wall with a black lace curtain blowing in the breeze. I knew I needed to get back to the club before Trix started looking for me. By now, it had to have been at least forty minutes since I went to the bathroom.

Shutting the door behind me, I went to make my way down the corridor when a heavy force slammed me into the wall beside the door. A whimper fell from my lips, but a hand quickly closed over them, stifling my yelp. I stared straight into a pair of chocolate brown eyes filled with pure

56

rage. Faust pressed me into the wall. His shoulders were shaking, and his jaw looked clenched so tight, I thought his teeth might break. Merrick was coming down the hall quickly once he spotted us. He held a gun in his hands, eyes shifting around the hallways.

Merrick looked murderous, too, but Faust spoke first, asking, "What the fuck were you thinking?!" His hand on my bicep tightened. "We gave you one rule, you stupid child. One simple rule. Stay where we can see you. Is this a fucking joke to you?!"

I tried to speak, but his other palm was still covering my mouth.

He shook his head. "I don't want to hear your excuses. We're done here. You're going home, and we'll be letting Mr. Harker know exactly what his daughter's been up to tonight."

My heart plummeted, but the sinking feeling only lasted a second as anger took its place. I shook my head, and to my relief, Faust let his palm fall away. I glared into his hate filled eyes. "Fuck you." I said it calmly through clenched teeth.

"C'mon, lass, let us get ya home," said Merrick from over Faust's shoulder. He no longer looked on edge and had stashed away his firearm. Actually, he sort of looked a little bored now, leaning against the far wall with his arms crossed over his chest leisurely.

Faust's gaze moved over my shoulder to my left, and his whole face tightened. He looked back at me. "Did you just come out of that room?" The question caught me off guard.

"What if I did?" I asked petulantly. "Let's just get—"

His nose went to my neck as he proceeded to breathe in deeply. My body locked up. What the fuck was he doing? Sniffing me? I squirmed, trying to pry his hands off, but it wasn't working. He was made of steel, immovable. Nose leaving the skin of my collar bone, Faust glared into my eyes, and for the first time since meeting him, I felt a lick of fear shoot down my spine. For a brief moment, I could have sworn I saw a bit of red in his brown eyes.

"What were you doing in that office? Do you have any idea how much danger you just put yourself in?" I didn't have it in me to tell him I didn't make the decision on my own. He narrowed his eyes. "This office belongs to the head of the Nocturne Coven, Serenity. You fucking smell like him." Surprisingly, he didn't say it with disgust. Just a fact.

"How could you possibly know that?" I asked, but my head was spinning, replaying what he just said.

The head of the Nocturne Coven. Atlas Nocturne. The ancient vampire who ran the bloodiest, fiercest, and oldest coven in the world. The man my father hated most in this world. *No.* It couldn't have been. There was no way he wouldn't have known it was me. I'd never seen his face before, as full blooded vampires didn't show up on cameras or in photographs, so I had no idea what the infamous Atlas looked like, but he'd know me. He had to have known, and yet he took me back here anyway.

"I didn't know," I whispered, shoulders deflating. Fuck, how could I have been so stupid? After everything that had happened, I told myself I'd be more careful. There were rumors that vampires had been behind the attack that killed Sean. Those rumors said it was a Nocturne vampire—one of Atlas' hitmen. Had I really been about to fuck my would be assassin? Or at least, the person who ordered my death?

Faust finally released me from the wall, and I almost sagged in relief. I was getting pretty tired of being manhandled. He stared down at me with an almost pitying look. "That's right, you don't know," he sneered. "You don't seem to know much of anything. I guess that's why your father asked us to babysit your stupid ass. You step out of line again, and stalking will seem like child's play, I promise you."

I practically choked on my own spit. I'd never in my life been spoken to like this aside from Carson or my father. Shoving my finger at his chest, I pressed in hard, but he didn't budge. "Who do you think you are, speaking to me like that?" I hissed. "I think you're mistaken, Faust. I'm *your* boss. I pay your salary, and I can have you fired just as easily, you fucking prick. Touch me again and I'll—"

"You'll what, princess?" he asked through a laugh. It was a bitter, unamused laugh, full of hate and darkness and seething irritation. "You'll do exactly what to me?" Our faces were inches apart, and his cruel smirk taunted my last nerve. "You couldn't even save your human brother. You didn't lift a finger to avenge the death of your own flesh and blood. Why should I be scared of a cowardly little girl?"

"Faust," Merrick cautioned. My watery eyes met his over Faust's shoulder. He was no longer leaning against the wall, but standing straight up, glaring at his friend. "We need to leave. This conversation should happen elsewhere."

"No," I said, pushing past Faust. "This conversation is over. I'm done with you." I stormed past them both, heading down the dark corridor, determined to get away and find Trix. I just wanted to get home, crawl into bed, and fall into a deep coma.

Dress shoes on the marble floor tapped along after me. "Oh, princess," Faust chuckled again, causing me to grit my teeth and walk even faster, not looking back. "We haven't even begun."

CHAPTER 4
SERENITY

Trix had left with Cade and Bryan on Merrick's orders. I'd scrolled through my phone the entire way back home, cringing as I read through her angry ranting texts. But I messaged her back, letting her know I was sorry and that I'd call her in the morning. Most importantly, I assured her I was safe.

We didn't call for Gregory at this late hour, since I didn't want to bother him during his time off with Kathy, so we took a taxi back to my family estate. It was an incredibly uncomfortable ride back and took nearly forty-five minutes weaving in and out of nighttime traffic. I sat there sandwiched between Faust and Merrick. They were huge men and took up way too much space, insisting on spreading out their legs on either side of me. I could barely breathe.

Faust had leaned away from me the entire time, brooding and glaring out the window like a child, which it suited me just fine. I was seriously contemplating putting in for a transfer, but I disregarded that notion quickly, knowing my father wouldn't give a shit if I didn't like my goon. If anything, he'd just have the man watch me even closer out of spite. Hell, I wouldn't be surprised if Faust was being paid specifically to be an asshole.

By the time we pulled up to my house, I was dead tired. I dragged my feet through the entryway, fighting another round of yawns, when a deep voice boomed through the room, sending dread pooling into my core. "A word, Serenity." Ryan Harker stood in front of a set of mahogany double doors that led down a hallway I spent most of my days avoiding. *Shit.* Back early. I should have known.

He had the lower right wing of the house outfitted for business, and I hadn't ventured there very often. But he was waiting now, glaring down at me with unreadable blue eyes that to all the world would have looked emotionless, but I knew better.

His eyes flickered over my shoulder, and he nodded. "You're dismissed for the night, gentlemen."

Silence. They didn't respond to my father, but I felt hesitance before Merrick and Faust turned away. I heard the taps of their dress shoes as they made their way down the hall, back the way we came. With every step they took, my emotions became more tumultuous. Not that I thought they would protect me from my own father, or that they had any inkling that protection would even be needed, but I suddenly felt naked and vulnerable. Without a word, Ryan turned on his heel and led me into his office.

The door barely had time to click shut before his fist hit my face. A direct impact. Blood flew from my lips, and I stumbled into the wall. My vision split. He'd hit me hard— hard enough that had I been human, a concussion might have been possible. Either that or death. I had a feeling he didn't care which.

"Look at you," he sneered, grabbing a fistful of my hair.

My head was wrenched backwards as his fingers tightened. "Did you think I wouldn't find out about your little trip to that filthy vampire club? Did you think I wouldn't know, you little whore?"

I whimpered as he dragged me by the hair on shaky feet until I was facing a massive gilded mirror hanging from his wall. He had my face pressed against the glass, smearing blood all over it.

"You're so much like your mother, do you know that, you dirty dhampir?" He spat the word. He hated what I was, and this was how he got revenge. "Spreading your legs for those monsters must make you feel special. Must make you feel like you're important, doesn't it?" He pressed me in harder. "Doesn't it!"

"Please!" I begged. I could feel the glass splintering under my cheek. I'd seen his rage grow over the past few months, but something about tonight just felt different.

Ryan chuckled in my ear, and the sound made my stomach roll. "You want to be fucked, Serenity? Is that what you really want?" There was too much glee in the question. My heart was suddenly thundering. The hand that wasn't pushing me into the mirror ran down my bare shoulder in a way that was decidedly not fatherly, and my whole body froze. My brain froze. My lungs. My heart. Everything went utterly still. "You want to know what a real man feels like, bitch? You don't have to run off to the vampires to get it. I can show you what a man feels like."

"Dad, please—"

A laugh ripped from his throat like a snarl. "*Dad, please*," he mocked before pressing his lips against my ear. "I'm not your father, Serenity. We've known it for some time now, but you just can't seem to let it sink in. You and I share no blood between us. You're nothing to me, do you know that? Nothing. I could slit your throat right here in this office and feel nothing."

"Do it, then," I choked out, feeling braver than I really was. "Just get it over with." Death would be far more preferable to what he had in mind. I didn't think my sanity could take it.

"And give you the easy way out?" He huffed. "You'd like that too much. No, I think I'd rather get my money's worth first. I've put up with your sniveling bitch of a mother for over twenty years, and it's time I got something out of it. It's time she atoned for the embarrassment she nearly caused me."

"Don't you touch her!" I barked, but was immediately rewarded with his fingers digging into my flesh as he pressed me harder into the mirror. By now, shards of glass were falling off in pieces, trickling to the floor with soft clinks.

He laughed again. "You stupid slut, I'm not going to touch Elodie. She is, after all, my wife. We have to look pretty for the cameras, don't we? But you, my dear, can serve so many other purposes."

"They'll know if you hurt me," I said. "They'll see the cuts and the bruises. They'll all know what a monster you really are, Ryan."

The moment I said his name, it was like something inside of him snapped. He spun me around so fast that the world seemed to spin, before tossing me to the floor. A kick to the ribs had me curling in on myself, trying my hardest to keep the vomit at bay. I lay there on the floor of his office, afraid to move a single muscle, but in the back of my mind, I knew all it would take for this to end right here was for me to unlock that cage. Let my monster free. It would be so easy. I could feel her simmering beneath my skin. She was waiting, biding her time. But I couldn't do it. I couldn't free her. I wasn't ready yet, and there was no way of knowing if I could reign her back in again. There were so many humans in this house...I couldn't risk it. So I let him come closer. Let him frighten me. Let him have all the power.

"You step out of line again, and I'll expose your mother for what she really is—a vamp fucker. I'll have her tossed to the streets and destitute, while you'll be locked away in the nearest psych ward. You'll never see the light of day again, Serenity." There was no room in his tone for questions. Just cold, dead truth. "That's not a threat. It's a promise."

I left his office, staggering down the hall and letting the heavy door shut behind me. The house was silent, and I wondered for a moment if I could get away with seeking out my mother. Then I thought better of it. She wouldn't want to see me. She'd just tell me to clean myself up and get to bed without anyone seeing me.

That was how Elodie always responded to another one of her husband's *episodes*, as she liked to call them. No matter how horrible he was or how many blows her body suffered under his fists, she stayed. Too prideful to take the shame of her infidelity and leave him. Too afraid of his retaliation. In truth, if she wanted to, she could leave the city. She could have taken me and fled when everything came to light. She could have chosen her daughter, but she didn't. I didn't think she ever would.

I made my way through the house on light feet, wincing when I swiped my tongue along my lip. A shallow cut was trying to knit itself back together, but it was slow going. I made it to my bedroom without running into anyone. My heart had been pounding the entire time, praying my new bodyguards wouldn't be there waiting for me. I had to admit, though, when I realized they were nowhere to be found, my heart sank a little. For some reason, I expected them to be waiting outside the door, and I didn't know what that said about me.

I showered, this time, sans tears. I was pretty much all cried out by now. Besides, I'd learned to take the physical pain by now. It was the other stuff that got to me. The feel of his hands on my body had me dry heaving under the steaming water. I'd scrubbed my skin until I felt like it was peeling off, and still, I felt dirty.

I spent a solid twenty minutes in there, staring at a straight razor in my shaking grip, wondering what it would feel like to run it across my veins. A simple slice, vertically should do it. A clean cut, severing tendons, veins, and flesh. A cut that would open me up and expel it all, allowing me to fade into nothingness. I could disappear into a place he could no longer find me. I stared at it. I even ran it along my skin a few times, watching the little blonde hairs fall away and wash down the drain.

I could do it. It would be so easy, and then I'd be free. It wasn't the first time I'd considered it. I couldn't count the times in the last twelve months I stood here in the same position, contemplating the same end. But I never did try. Call me a coward or call me a fool. I didn't know what to call myself. But I was getting closer and closer to making that cut. Closer to the edge of my sanity. Closer to the brink of sweet oblivion. Perhaps the only thing holding me back was the thought of the what-ifs. What if I didn't die? What if it didn't work? I was a dhampir. Half-vampire, half-human.

What if the cut left me weak, but didn't complete the job? Could I go the rest of my life with that on my conscience? I didn't know the answer. So maybe that was what stilled my hand and had me toweling off, climbing into bed, and surviving another night.

Chapter 5
Serenity

*M*y bed felt like sandpaper, and it took hours to fall asleep that night. Hours of staring up at my ceiling, wondering what the hell I was supposed to tell Carson. His dinner party was in the afternoon, and though I healed fast, I knew my lips would be swollen and probably too noticeable to be covered with makeup. He'd be furious. Not furious at Ryan for hitting me, but he'd be furious at me for prompting him to lose his temper in the first place.

It was nearing the afternoon already. I'd skipped all of my classes and stayed beneath the covers, watching my phone blow up on my nightstand. Eventually, I texted Trix and told her I was sick. She called bullshit, but I never responded. I hated lying to her. She was probably the one person in the world I could trust with my new secret. Being a darkling rights activist, she of all people would sympathize with my plight. Never in a million years would my cousin betray me. It would have to be soon. I needed an ally.

Around six o'clock, I pulled myself out of bed and got to

work on my hair and makeup. Carson texted me, saying he'd have a car pick me up in an hour, ever punctual. The dress he'd sent over wasn't to my taste at all, so I waited until the very last second to put it on. Tonight, he had me in a pale pink lace monstrosity. Something way too short for my liking, with little capped sleeves and a fluttery skirt. I looked like a doll. As requested, I'd left my hair down, long and wavy, the way he liked it. My lips were a baby pink, and my eyes were shimmering lightly with a nude eyeshadow and some light brown mascara. Carson liked the natural look, said bold makeup was for whores and vamps, so I had to be careful.

I didn't feel like myself at all as I stood in front of the standing mirror next to my closet. Twisting and turning, I bit back a groan as my eyes ran over the fakeness of it all. Then I smiled and smoothed down the fabric. Underneath the pale pink was something just for me. Something I promised myself Carson would not be seeing tonight, no matter how much he begged.

The clock was ticking, and it was go time. My makeup covered what I could, but I didn't have a makeup artist today. I hoped the lighting was dim during dinner at least. I was done stalling, so I headed for the door, but I hadn't counted on Faust being directly on the other side. He was standing there against the wall with his hands folded in front of him, looking bored, but the very instant he saw me, something that looked like murder flashed across his face.

"What happened to your face?" he spat.

Shit. "Mind your business, Grumpy. Let's go." I continued to make my way down the hall with him on my heels. I didn't want to face him. In the back of my head, I knew one of them would notice right away. I was fooling myself thinking I could pass these cuts off.

"Serenity, stop." His hand on my shoulder had me stumbling to a halt. I kept forgetting how strong he was. My mind flashed back to yesterday when he had me pressed up against the wall at Rue. "You're going to answer my question before we go any farther. What happened to your face? Why is your lip three sizes too big?"

I stared at him like he was the world's biggest idiot. It didn't take a genius to put two and two together. "I guess they don't require a college degree to become a bodyguard, do they?" He frowned, so I kept on. "Let's just say dear old dad wasn't too happy about last night and leave it at that. Don't worry about me. I'm used to it."

"The senator did that to you?" he asked, voice low and slightly trembling. I didn't know why he bothered to pretend he cared. Indecision and confusion crossed his expression next, like he couldn't figure out if he should be concerned or not.

I scoffed. "You have a lot of catching up to do." I turned from him, but once again, he just grabbed me by the arm, hauling me back around until we were face to face. "You have boundary issues, Faust. Anyone ever tell you that? You're supposed to guard me, not manhandle me."

I could tell my words were flying right over his head. "Does this happen often?" he asked. In his voice was a silent rage, but he was doing a really good job at keeping it under control. Our faces were too close together for comfort, but at least our words were silent enough so as to not alert the staff.

"I don't owe you any sort of explanation, but you'll find out for yourself if you manage to last long enough. My father is many things, but a family man isn't one of them. Get with the program and stop trying to make me late." We just stared at each other for a few tense moments, his jaw clenched tight, until I heard footsteps from down the hall.

"There's a car here for you, Miss Harker," Merrick's deep voice boomed in the tense silence.

Faust still had a hold of my arms, and I felt his fingers flex. He was biting back words, and for some reason, I almost wished he'd just spit them out. Who was he to judge me or my family? Who was he to take the moral high ground here? Surely I wasn't the only rich, spoiled little princess getting knocked around by her father. Surely he had to have suspected. But just like all the rest, I knew he'd do nothing.

Turning away, I was surprised when Faust let me go so easily. The spot where his fingers had been burned ice cold once more, catching me off guard. If I hadn't already seen both him and Merrick walking around in the open sunlight, I'd have assumed they were vampires. Merrick was watching me with a raised eyebrow and a perplexed expression that I couldn't place, but I just swept right past him. I did, however, see the way his eyes narrowed in on my bottom lip. They didn't miss much.

I made my way through the house, not bothering to say anything to my parents before leaving. My mother already knew I had plans with Carson tonight, and I knew she wouldn't do anything to stop it. I wished Gregory was the one who was dropping me off at the Badgley estate, but of course, Carson had to send his own car. Just another show of force and power he didn't have to flex for me to realize it. He didn't send a limo but a regular town car, and I grumbled inwardly, knowing I was about to be once again sandwiched between my two goons.

The ride to the Badgley estate didn't take long. He lived

on the outer edge of the city between the wildlands and pack territory. His family owned acres of land that they'd turned into a massive golf course, and even squinting into the setting sun, I couldn't see the end of it.

Merrick and Faust said nothing the whole drive over, but there was a tense silence between the three of us, something unspoken, and I knew they were silently fuming. I didn't think they were mad on my behalf. I wasn't under some misplaced notion that they were angry at my getting the shit kicked out of me, but rather that they hadn't known about it. These two seemed like control freaks that way, and perhaps the fact that things were happening behind the scenes was pissing them off. That, and the fact that I refused to talk about it.

Merrick helped me out of the car, and I let him. I was aching all over from the moment I woke up, and I wasn't too proud to take help, even from someone I was already beginning to loathe. His fingers wrapped around mine, squeezing slightly, and the pressure was surprisingly comforting. He let go just as quickly, and I could have sworn that right before I turned, I saw him wipe his palm on his slacks. My cheeks flamed while I tried to discreetly wipe my own hands on my dress in case I really was a sweaty mess.

Carson lived in a massive house made of red brick and steepled roofs. It was an old home, surrounded by rose gardens and gaudy looking water fountains. There was a guest house around the back that was larger than some middle income single family homes. The front double door opened, and Carson stepped out. He wore yet another one of his badly fitted tan suits. I really hated his strange desire to wash himself out. The color aged him and it was unfortunate, because he really was a handsome bastard.

Carson's watery eyes roved my face, and like Merrick and Faust, landed on my swollen lip. But instead of asking if I was okay or if I was hurt or needed medical attention, he seemed unbothered. Perhaps my father called ahead and warned him to expect it. Perhaps he blamed my impairment on something I'd done at Rue.

Oh, fuck. Does Carson know about that? I hadn't checked social media this morning, but that was the only way anyone could have found out so fast. My father followed social media closely. He was on Twitter every day, searching his own hashtags and constantly Googling himself. The Senator was vain, and I should have known he'd be the first to know about my not so secretive trip into 'enemy territory.'

Carson wrapped his arm around my shoulders and led me into the house, and it took all the willpower I had in my body not to shrug out of his embrace. Once again, a cloud of cologne enveloped me and I struggled to breathe. I didn't know what his fascination was with dousing himself in chemical scents, but it was repulsive. Not anything like the smell of leather and smoke that reminded me of Atlas...

No, I wouldn't go there. The image of his face, his hands, and his lips had haunted my dreams last night. I shivered just thinking about the feel of my tongue running over his sharp teeth. It was almost laughable to think I'd pulled any sort of pleasure from fucking Carson the other day in the wake of what Atlas had done to me. The even funnier thing was that we hadn't even gotten around to having sex. He'd eaten me out, and it was heaven and hell all wrapped into one. I could probably go the rest of my life and never feel that thrill again.

Carson didn't acknowledge Merrick and Faust. He didn't even seem to notice they were there. But that was just how men like him were trained and bred. Anyone that worked for them was the help. They were beneath him and unimportant, no different than the coffee table or a kitchen utensil. But they followed closely, and strangely, their presence calmed me a little. Carson always made me feel uneasy and on edge. You just never knew when his temper would flare and he'd become a different person entirely. But with these two huge men backing me up, I was sure I'd walk out of this dinner party unscathed.

He led us into the opulent, old money dining room where six people sat waiting. My stomach dipped uncomfortably. I didn't recognize anyone in the room. They were all men—some older, maybe in their fifties, while three of them looked young like Carson. They were each impeccably dressed in their expensive suits and watches that cost more than most people's homes, and each held a scotch or a brandy in their hands.

Eyes crawled all over me as I was ushered in with Carson's hand on my lower back. The heat of his skin was an uncomfortable burning, and I couldn't help but compare the touch to Faust and his coolness that had shocked me at first. Peeking at Faust, he immediately circled the long dinner table, eyeing each of the men in the room, but showed no hint of emotion on his face. He scanned them as I was placed in a chair at the head of the room. I couldn't look away from that focus.

It was strange. Out in the car, I'd wanted to be as far away from Merrick and Faust as possible. They were the enemy, hired by my father most likely against their will. Back in the car, the animosity between us was thick, but in this room, they felt like my only allies. Situational allies, I guessed you could say.

The men were still observing me blatantly as I pretended to get settled. The table was set with expensive dinnerware made of silver and goblets to match. There were glasses for water, for club soda and champagne, and there were separate glasses for wine and tumblers for the harder stuff. Forks and knives had been spread out on either side of the plate—the only way to dine with affluence.

I could feel Merrick's presence behind me, and it grounded me a little. Carson made his way around the other side of the table and took a seat. It was times like this I was happy Carson was so strict about following decorum. It was seen as impolite to sit next to your spouse or significant other. At least propriety was my saving grace tonight.

"You've never met my colleagues," Carson began. He snapped his fingers, and a young woman in a maid's uniform bustled out of the kitchen doors with a bottle of wine, then promptly filled his glass. He gestured to the older men on the left hand side. "Reginald Casey and his son, Dameon."

I looked at the man in question. Reginald was a plump Caucasian man with thinning russet hair and blue eyes that might have twinkled in his youth. His face, however, was stony and greasy. Ugly. His son sat across from him to my right, and it was a struggle to hold his gaze. Partially because he was too busy ogling my breasts. I didn't say a word. I didn't tell them it was nice to meet them or bother to give them my name back. Carson wouldn't want that. He'd want me to keep my mouth shut while he put on a show. I kept my face carefully blank.

"This is Roger and Michael Bleu and their sons, Timothy and Lyle." I looked at the two other older men. They looked remarkably similar to one another. Both had muddy brown hair, brown eyes, and tawny skin with crow's feet. The one on the left had thick framed glasses that magnified his eyes too much. He did look slightly familiar, though I couldn't place him. Their sons looked similar, just younger, so I guessed these four were a family of sorts. Fathers and sons and cousins.

"I assume my Serenity needs no introduction," he said through a chuckle, like he'd been exceptionally clever. *My Serenity*, he'd said. Mine. That was what I was to him—an object.

A round of polite chuckles from the men had me squirming uncomfortably. Without thought, my eyes shot up and met Faust's gaze. His stare burned a hole into my flesh. I could tell he was on edge, but he never looked away. There were so many things I wished I could communicate through my eyes alone. I wished I could tell him to create some sort of emergency so that we could leave this place. I didn't like the way Carson's friends made me feel like a pig on display.

"Ah, just in time," Carson said as the tapping of dress shoes filled the room.

My eyes shot to the empty space at the table. How had I missed that? I was exceptionally unobservant tonight. I blamed it on the unwavering attention of my perplexing bodyguards. The tapping drew nearer, and when Ryan Harker walked into the room, I nearly choked on the small sip of water I'd been in the process of swallowing. Our eyes locked from across the room, and his thin lips curled up on the side. Those blue eyes shone with an evil I'd never really seen in them before. Suddenly, it was like being back in his office again, with his body pressed up against my back as he whispered unholy things in my ear, making me feel small and helpless and worthless. Shivers rolled down my spine. Shivers of dread.

I couldn't figure out what he was doing here. Why on earth would he be interested in a small dinner party at

Carson Badgley's house? Carson and Ryan never really interacted outside of family dinners. Usually, Carson's father was present during those times, but he was suspiciously absent tonight. Ryan took a seat and wasted no time pouring himself some scotch. My throat was thick with him in the room.

Once again, I searched out Faust, but this time, he wasn't looking at me. His eyes were on Ryan, intently. It was a good thing the senator was unconcerned with my goons, because the look Faust was giving him right now would get him almost immediately fired and probably taken out back and beaten bloody before sending him to the unemployment line. His square jaw was so tight, it looked painful. He was still in a nearly unnatural way and barely breathing, it seemed.

"Now that we're all here," Carson said, clapping once, the sound cracking like a whip through the room, "let's eat."

Two maids came out of the kitchen doors again, holding silver platters which they set down in front of each of us. I could already smell the red meat wafting from underneath the lids, making my mouth water, but when a tray arrived in front of me, I just blinked at it. Blinked slowly as the maid removed the covering. It took me a moment to realize that my steak was almost completely rare. Barely even warm. Blood pooled around it on the plate, enough that if I poured it into a wine glass, it would fill it to the brim.

I looked at Carson and he just watched me, sipping from his glass of red wine. He raised an eyebrow as if daring me to open my mouth. He was fucking with me, trying to provoke a reaction out of me in front of all his friends. Well, I wouldn't give him one. I wasn't here to play games tonight. I just wanted to suffer through this meal in silence like the pretty little trophy he wanted me to be.

Someone in the room cleared their throat. "Your speech at the museum was inspiring," said a gruff voice. The older man across from me was looking at my fath—at Ryan. "Drew quite the crowd."

The senator smiled with no real emotion, swirling the amber liquid around in his glass. "I'd expect nothing less." Always so full of himself.

"I spotted several mongrels among the crowd," interjected the younger man introduced as Dameon. "Spies, do doubt. But they were dealt with swiftly." Those wolves I thought I saw in the crowd that day. Mongrels, they called them, a disgusting name. I rolled my eyes.

"They were spying on a live streamed press conference?" I asked incredulously before I could shut myself up. *Shit shit shit shit!*

The room went silent, and all eyes went to me. Ryan's face was blank, but Carson, he looked murderous. I was supposed to sit here with my mouth shut and look pretty. No talking, much less questioning one of his friends in the presence of the others. Fuck, I'd be paying for that little slip up later. The men ignored me. Pretended like I hadn't even spoken. It was disgusting, the way they dismissed females. Very old school and outdated to expect the wives and girlfriends to keep their mouths shut and legs open at all times. I knew I wouldn't let this be the endgame for me. I wouldn't end up like my mother, who practically sold herself to Ryan Harker in exchange for money, fame, and her face on television.

Ever since finding out about the affair she'd had, the one that resulted in me, I wondered who my father really was and what it was about him that convinced Elodie Harker to put everything on the line for him. He must have been a special man to break her like that. But what sort of man up and leaves the second they find out they're about to have a child? Not a man at all, though, I kept reminding myself. Not in the traditional sense. He wasn't really a man, he was a vampire. Who knew how old my father was, or how many concubines he'd collected over the years or decades. Maybe even centuries. Was my mother just one in a long line of willing blood bags?

The thought curdled my stomach. I tried to keep its contents down as I zoned out of the conversation entirely. The men were discussing campaign strategy and the possibilities of voter suppression. They were cheaters and liars, the lot of them. They schemed and plotted, knowing that if they were to intervene in voting halls near the Nocturne District and the pack lands, they could cheat their way through the election.

Ryan had a rival this year. It was announced some months ago that he would no longer be running unopposed for the position he'd held for over a decade. And to top it all off, this candidate was a witch, pissing Ryan off and starting another race war in the streets of Nocturne and Nightingale, the home of the witches and warlocks.

Humans didn't think darklings had the right to positions of power, but the Coexist Doctrine said otherwise. It was a constant tug of war, but the witch community was holding strong. Their candidate was a woman named Estelle Nightengale, who was matron of the city's largest clan. She was a stoic, sharp sort of woman, with flaming red hair and a severe face but an engaging personality. She was loud and proud and not afraid to challenge Ryan on every single subject. She debated with the best of them, and I'd never have the guts to say it out loud, but I'd been silently cheering her on for the better part of the last year. Trix was a big fan and loved to let everyone know it. I wasn't going to lie, I'd be voting for her in this coming election.

The men talked shit about Estelle, calling her every name in the book. Whore. Imposter. Monster, or worse, an abomination. That was what they called darkling women. A derogatory term, but they slung it around the table among laughter and long pulls of their scotch, brandy, and wine. Once again, my stomach curdled. They were insufferable. I'd never understand what made these pot bellied, sweaty, pockmark-faced men think they were in any way superior to the darklings.

Faust looked uncomfortable when I glanced up at him, and It made me pause. His eyes were on Carson, boring a hole into the side of my boyfriend's face. Though his face held no visible expression, his eyes told another story— murder, that's what those dark eyes spoke. I watched Faust from under my lashes as discreetly as I could, and I wished for a moment that Merrick had joined him on that side of the room so I could watch him too.

I didn't get why Faust was having this reaction to Carson's words and Ryan's jabs. He looked on edge and a split second away from snapping someone's neck. As far as I knew, both Faust and Merrick were human men. They could walk in the sun and be perfectly fine, and their skin was tan and flushed like a human. They held no magical aura around them the way witches did. They also weren't wolves, I'd be able to smell them if that were the case. So why did he care so much?

Dinner came to an end, and I brushed away my barely touched plate. I could barely stomach the too rare steak. The blood wasn't the sort I wanted or needed. It was dead blood and not appetizing in the slightest. Quite the opposite, in fact. Carson didn't comment, just flicked his eyes from the plate to my face with a sly grin. He'd known I wouldn't touch it. I didn't know how much he'd told these other men about me, so I wasn't sure if they were in on his little joke or not, but it made me want to punch him right in the teeth.

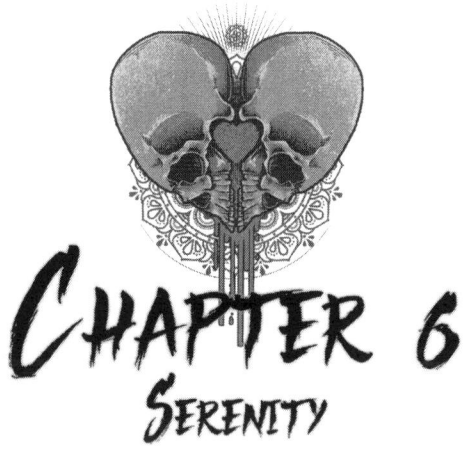

CHAPTER 6
SERENITY

"*L*et's retire to the sitting room," Carson suggested. It was a struggle to contain my eye roll.

I knew their habits better than I knew my own. Now we'd all file into a stuffy room, where Carson would break out the fancy booze and the imported cigars. Then they'd all sit around and have a long discussion about how awesome they all were. Or perhaps they'd talk shit about their wives and girlfriends, lamenting the fact that they were forced to put up with them at all. Sometimes, I wondered why they didn't just fuck each other and save themselves the headache.

I wished I could just leave. I wanted to get back home so I could vent my frustration to Trix. I decided it was time I came clean and just told her the whole truth. All these feelings and uncertainties were piling up inside me, and I didn't know if I could last much longer on my own. I always prided myself on being independent and self-sufficient, but it was too much, all of it. Finding out I wasn't human changed things. Changed my life, how I saw the world, and how I saw myself. I not only lost my entire identity, I also lost a father and a brother and any hope I had for a normal future.

I was looking forward to hearing what Trix had to say about it all, especially advice about handling these cravings...and not just for blood. But most of all, I just looked forward to sliding that weight off of my shoulders for the first time in months—the longest twelve months of my entire twenty-four years.

I followed behind the men like a good little bitch, a shackled woman with no freedom of her own. No voice and no opinions. Ryan walked past me, and we brushed shoulders. I cringed back, slamming my shoulder into the wall to avoid touching him. I heard him chuckle under his breath. When he looked at me, it made me feel like vomiting up the bloody steak I just picked at.

For twenty plus years, that man had been my father. My dad. Someone I didn't much like, but reluctantly said I loved. I was beginning to realize that the love I thought I felt for him wasn't real. It was an obligation. I'd loved him because I thought he was my father, and so blood ties meant more than my disapproval of how he handled business. I may not have agreed with his beliefs, but I'd been able to turn a blind eye to it all for the sake of family.

Now I realized I was just a foolish girl with her head in the sand. I should've realized I was nothing like the man that barely even raised me. He was never around when I needed him. He didn't do any of the things fathers do for their daughters. I was raised by staff mostly. But it still hurt, looking at him now. Every time we locked eyes, my skin hurt from the phantom bruises that were long healed. I could remember the impact of every blow he'd rained down on me in the months following Sean's death. He blamed me for it. Blamed me for the fact that his real child was no longer with us. Sometimes, I blamed me too.

I sat on a lonely chaise lounge towards the door while the men situated themselves on cherry brown leather sofas. The room was stuffy and smelled like leather and ash. It was too warm, and the fire in the fireplace was stifling. I sat on the plush velvet with my hands folded in my lap demurely, just trying to shut the fuck up for as long as I possibly could. I didn't want any more trouble tonight.

Merrick stood by the far door with his hands clasped in front of him. His shoulders were broad and tense. He stared straight forward, his hard green eyes seemingly vacant, but I knew better. He was acutely aware of every single thing happening in this room. I tested him a little when I went to shift my leg over my knee. The moment my skin brushed the velvet cushion, Merrick flinched almost imperceptibly and then forcibly straightened his shoulders again. I hid a smirk.

Faust was now on the other side of the room, watching Merrick. I could have sworn I saw a small eye roll, but I couldn't be sure. He refused to look at me, though. For some reason, it bothered me. I didn't know why I felt like this around my bodyguards. They were throwing me off my groove these past two days, and I couldn't figure out why. They were definitely more invasive than the last ones I'd had. Thinking about it, I honestly couldn't even recall speaking more than a few sentences to my previous goons, and when I did, it was mostly just directions or requests.

I'd zoned out, and now the men were lighting up cigars. Carson picked up a small black remote from the coffee table in the center of the room and dimmed the lights with it. The room was cast in a romantic glow, but instead of putting me at ease, it made me sweat. As I zoned back in, I noticed their conversation had come to a halt and the young men kept glancing over at me from the corner of their eyes. I even got a look from the older man with the thick glasses that made me feel slimy. They thought they were being sly, but I could feel every lick of their eyes over my bare skin.

"Come here, Serenity," Carson beckoned, and I stiffened. His voice was deceptively soft and croony, like one would use when speaking with a child.

I hesitated, uncrossing my legs as my body jolted forward on instinct to heed his summons. It was automatic. Years of conditioning had my body moving before I could tell myself this was an odd request. Carson gave me a sharp, narrow eyed gaze that had me standing slowly, brushing the nonexistent lint off of my pale pink dress. I caught Ryan's grin as he lounged back on the sofa. His coat was unbuttoned, and in his grasp was an empty glass.

For some reason, I looked to Faust as I took a step. His eyes were on me now, but they didn't alleviate the fluttering in my stomach. I just made my way over to my boyfriend, my heels clicking in the silence of the room.

"Stop," Carson said suddenly. I jerked to a halt in the center of the room, right in between the two sofas full of men. "Right there's fine, baby doll."

Gritting my teeth, I resisted the urge to tell him to shut the fuck up like I had the other night. But right now wasn't the time to take risks. I was in a snake pit, and I needed to tread carefully.

"Do a little spin for me," he said. I detected a hint of a smile in his liquid voice.

"What?" I asked. I didn't understand. He wanted me to...spin?

"Don't argue with me." The humor in his eyes vanished, replaced with shards of ice. "Spin, Serenity. Now."

"I-I don't get it..."

"Do as you're told," Ryan said. He still reclined against the sofa, eyes hooded and mouth in a tight line. His jacket was now completely off, exposing just a white dress shirt with the sleeves rolled up. How had I not noticed him remove his jacket?

Biting my tongue against any arguments I might've given them, I stifled my pride and my embarrassment, and spun. It was a slow movement. Steady, but slow. My cheeks were probably flaming red, but I made a full revolution, making a point to avoid meeting Merrick or Faust's eyes. I couldn't believe I was being forced to show myself off like chattel to these men. It was barbaric and disgusting.

I could physically feel their eyes on my naked flesh, and I wished Carson had let me be the one to pick out tonight's outfit. A turtleneck sweater and some parachute pants were sounding pretty good right about now. I was realizing that a lot of forethought had gone into tonight, from my dress, to my hair, to the time and company. Carson had planned this weeks ago at least.

"Marvelous, isn't she?" Carson asked. A few responding mumbles of affirmation filled the room. He chuckled. "Feel free to take a closer look, gentlemen." Those words rattled around in my brain for a moment. I couldn't quite grasp onto them. My stomach bottomed out, and my heart shriveled into a prune.

Get a closer look...

A closer look at me—my body.

I suddenly felt a very real shiver of fear snake down my spine. Something wasn't right. Something was off. It seemed I was the last one in the know at this dinner party...if that was even what this was. I didn't know anymore. Carson was acting weird. In the past, he'd always enjoyed showing off his trophy girlfriend...but never like this.

I heard the squeaking of leather and the tapping of dress shoes on the marble floor as I made another revolution. I came to a stop, facing the men as two of the younger ones approached. They both still held glasses of scotch in their hands and cigars dangled lazily from their mouths as their eyes ran over me. Lust filled their gazes, blatant, uninhibited lust. I could feel it crawling over me like spiders I couldn't shake off. I just had to stand there and let them look. And god, I hoped looking was all they'd do. Every one of my instincts told me to make a run for it, to leave the room and leave the estate and never look back. Every instinct told me I was in danger, incredible danger. I didn't know what to do.

This time, I did look up at Faust across the room. He was a little closer to us than before, no longer standing against the wall. He was nearing the back of the sofa and frowning deeply, seemingly biting the inside of his cheek. I could tell it was bothering him, what my boyfriend was making me do. Not to mention the fact that to him and Merrick, Ryan over there, witnessing all of this, was still my father. I could see the indecision in Faust's brown eyes, but I shook my head slightly, pleading with him not to act. If he did, this would get very ugly, very fast.

"How old did you say this one was?" one of the older men asked.

This one. This one? What on earth was he talking about?

"Turned twenty-four in February of this year," said Carson.

Someone made a clucking sound with their tongue. "I would have guessed younger. Pity."

My stomach lurched, and I looked at Carson pleadingly.

"Carson, what's going on?" This had to be a joke. It just fucking had to be.

"Shut your mouth, Serenity. The adults are speaking," he said in a bored voice.

He stood and walked towards me. The younger men made room for him, backing up, but not far enough for my liking. Carson reached out, pinching a lock of pale hair between his fingers before glancing at the other men. "She's not out of her prime quite yet, boys. On the contrary, she's quite pliable yet. Feel free to—"

"Carson?" I asked in a panic.

My head whipped to the side from an unexpected blow. Cheek stinging and eyes watering, I held my burning skin and looked at my boyfriend in shock. He'd never hit me in front of anyone before. Never. In fact, he'd always gone out of his way to play the doting boyfriend in public. Until now, apparently. I was right—something was very wrong.

I heard movement and the click of a weapon. Faust was nearly around the back of the couch, gun in hand and ready to draw on Carson, when Ryan stood up.

"Stand down," he told my bodyguard. He looked over my shoulder next, eyeing Merrick, who I assumed was also holding his gun at the ready.

I saw Faust hesitate. Stopping dead in his tracks, he frowned deeply, staring at Ryan now. "Sir?" he asked.

"I said stand down. Get back over by the wall and don't move until I instruct you otherwise." There was a clear note of challenge in his tone. Like he could tell Faust was on edge. Ryan never once questioned his own power and knew the men would heed his warnings no matter what.

With hesitation, Faust backed up, holstering his weapon inside his suit jacket. His eyes flickered to mine, and I was mortified when I realized tears were building in mine, preparing to slide down my cheeks in hot, salty trails. I blinked them away before he could tell they were red.

I stood stock still as Ryan approached, looking me over as one would a car in a fancy lot. My whole body rejected the way his eyes drank me in. It was unnatural still, despite knowing he wasn't actually my father. It was disgusting and repulsive to even entertain.

I flinched when a clammy hand brushed my upper arm. Limbs turning to stone, I closed my eyes tight. Fingers brushed my arm, skimming down my bicep, my elbow, and wrist, before making its way back up toward my collar bone. I was fighting a gag. I didn't know whose hand it was, I just knew it didn't belong anywhere near my body.

"So soft," a low voice murmured. There was an answering chuckle. "Is she a virgin?" the same one asked.

Oh gods...

"Unfortunately, no. Not a virgin, not by a long shot. I can personally attest to that," said Carson.

My eyes flew open, and I saw the man with the glasses frown, his mouth turning down in what would be comical in any other situation but this one.

"But I can assure you, Congressman, she's a gem. Suitable for the task and then some."

What was he fucking talking about? Task? What task? My head was spinning. And...congressman? I looked the man over once more. How hadn't I seen it before? I should have known right away. Oh gods, this was bad. So fucking bad.

"I want to leave," I whispered. Barely a sound fell from my lips, but I knew they could all hear me. I met Carson's eyes. "Carson, please. I want to go home."

His thin lips flattened into a grim line, and the laughter in his eyes once again faded to steel. The man looking out at me from that handsome face wasn't the same boy I grew up with. There was a time I would have called Carson a friend. A good boy. A loyal companion. Back when the world hadn't jaded us. Back before his father got his hooks into him. But I saw not a single drop of that man in the eyes staring back at me right now.

Fingers slithered into my hair, yanking my head back, and I stumbled. My head was still sore from the way Ryan had grabbed me last night, and pain throbbed all the way down my neck. Hot breath hit my ear, and despite myself, I let out a pained whimper.

"If you don't keep your mouth shut, whore, I'll shut it for you permanently. You don't need teeth for what we have in store for this body."

A sob slipped past my lips. A sob and a suppressed gag. I locked eyes with Faust yet again, and from here, it looked like he was visibly shaking. His eyes were murderous, and he kept glancing at Merrick. I could tell they were communicating with their eyes somehow, trying to decide what to do about this. I knew they were fighting an internal battle. Ryan Harker was their boss, and I was just their charge. There was a clear line they weren't supposed to cross.

"Don't worry, little Serenity," Carson crooned. My head was still wrenched sideways as Ryan held me by the hair like a fucking animal. "You'll serve your purpose soon enough. Though, I am genuinely sorry it couldn't be as my wife. You would have looked fucking delectable by my side. The cameras simply don't do you justice. But, in light of certain... revelations, it's come to my attention that your services are needed elsewhere." His smile made me sick.

Ryan's hand crept down my side, fingertips burning into my flesh. I held my breath as those fingers reached the bottom hem of my dress. Oh, fuck, I was going to throw up.

It was coming up my throat, burning, and my mouth filled with acid.

Yep. There it was... I vomited, projectile style. Every single one of the men around me jumped backwards with a curse, even Ryan. He wrenched away from me and even tore a few strands of my hair out when it caught on his ring. I paid no attention to the pain as something came over me then. As I heaved the meager amounts of dinner I forced down my throat onto the floor, I made a decision. A decision that would change everything, but it was mine. And I needed to do it fast.

I spit on the ground, turning around in a fluid motion, and ran for the door to the far left. There was nobody guarding it, and I moved just a little too fast to be completely human. Even though I was nowhere near as strong or fast as someone like myself should have been, I was still able to get out of the room before anyone could act. After all, there was a huge pool of steaming vomit on the floor between me and the men.

I shoved my way through the door, slamming it behind me. Cursing, footsteps, and shouts rang out from the other side. I kicked off my heels before I went any farther, running into a maid as I went. She slammed into the wall, and the tray she was holding clattered to the ground, glass shattering in my wake. Good. It might slow them down even more.

I made for the front door, lucky I'd memorized Carson's house a long time ago. Luckily, there were no goons posted at the entrance. Once again, Carson Badgley was too full of himself and thought himself a god among men, underestimating anyone he came in contact with. I slammed out the front door and into the night. The gravel under my feet tore at the soles, ripping into my flesh, but I could scarcely feel it. I didn't care. I just needed to run.

A sudden wave of adrenaline came over me then. I had no idea where it came from, but it was like my body filled with a burst of speed and energy I'd never felt before. Tears streamed out of my eyes. I couldn't stop. I wouldn't stop, not for anyone or anything. Having no idea what to do or where to go, I ran through the open gates and dashed down the dark street of the affluent neighborhood. I could have run into the woods around the side of the house and disappeared, but I knew that there was an electric fence that ran the line of the Badgley property, specifically put there to keep the wolves off of their land.

I could hear barking, chilling the blood in my veins. Barking and shouting. Behind me, the floodlights the Badgley's also had set up around their estate lit up, casting the whole neighborhood in nearly daylight levels of brightness, but I kept going. I ran down the street barefoot, sobbing and bleeding, looking like a crazy person, but I never stopped. Not once. Not as cars passed and honked their horns. Not as an elderly woman walking her little dog shuffled to the side of the sidewalk with her hand on her heart and an expression of terror on her face.

I had tunnel vision. Escape. Escape now. Leave this place. Get away from the men who wanted to hurt me. Who wanted to use me. I didn't know what for, but nothing about the way they'd been sizing me up promised anything good. I ran for twenty minutes, still listening to the howling of Carson's hunting hounds, but they were growing quieter. I was fast, faster than any human had any right to be, but I wasn't human. I wasn't strong, but I wasn't human.

Up ahead through the darkness was a large bridge that crossed the harbor. On the other side was a suburb outcropping of humans who didn't want to live the inner city life. *Fuck*. Had I really run that far? I had to be miles away from Carson's house. Good.

I made for the bridge and started to slow. It probably wasn't a good idea to slow down, because when I did, an overwhelming surge of pain came over me. I could feel the sting of gravel under my bleeding feet and the bruising on the back of my head from Ryan's death grip. Sobs ripped from my throat as I stumbled. I coughed and sputtered, dry heaving while I fought to keep moving.

Once on the bridge, I kept to the side where a metal railing was the only thing preventing someone from walking right off. I made it to the middle of the bridge before I stopped. Wind whipped my hair around my face, and it stung. In the distance were the rolling black waves of the harbor. The bridge was extremely tall. One of the tallest, most massive structures in all of Noc City. It was a relatively new structure, as the old bridge was nothing more than an underwater tunnel leading from one mass of land to the other. This one was truly a marvel.

I stood there, gripping onto the cold railing, just as it started to rain. During all my running, I'd failed to scent the change in the weather on the wind. It sprinkled lightly at first, gradually building until the smell of it mixed with the briny salt smell of the sea. Waves sloshed far below me, but looked pitch black, cresting up into foamy whitecaps that undulated in the steadily rising wind.

As I watched the water, my mind began to swirl with possibilities. Not many possibilities. Two possibilities really. They were so clear suddenly. The water was so inviting, so undulating and tumultuous, just like my heart. As black as my soul and as deadly as the monster that hid inside me. Suddenly, I knew what I needed to do. I knew exactly how to get away from Ryan and Carson and every man who thought he ruled my life. I suddenly had an out. A real out. It was all so clear now.

I'd obviously contemplated suicide many times, though I never went through with it. It always seemed like something *other* people did. Sad people who lost the will to live, or who, having no other choice, took the easy way out. I'd thought them cowards or crazies. I'd thought them weak and unstable...but were they? Were they really? Or were they simply as trapped as I was?

I could see it so clearly now. My way out. Just a simple step. One easy step. It would be smoother than breathing. I'd plunge into the icy cold water, hitting it fast enough to shatter every bone in my body. I could do it. So, so fucking easily. And I'd finally be free. No more pain. No more guilt. No more...

I hadn't even noticed, but I was suddenly on the other side of the railing, holding onto it with my back pressed against the cold metal. My pale pink dress fluttered in the wind, and my white hair whipped around my head, tangling and slapping against my raw skin. Tears dripped down my face, staining the collar of my dress a deep red. I could vaguely make out the sounds of cars honking their horns, but not a single person stopped. Nobody really cared. I didn't blame them.

The world went utterly still. Sounds muted until all I could hear was the beating of my own heart, slow and steady. A smile curled my lips as the prospect of freedom really sunk in. I embraced it. Finally, I was going to be free and it would be my choice. I was the master of my own destiny. Fuck them all. Fuck the world, and fuck this life. I was done with it. I was ready to move on to whatever came next.

I let myself lean forward, hands reaching back and gripping the railing loosely. My body was hovering over the rolling sea, and I whispered my thanks to the blackness. Thank you for freeing me when I was too weak to do it myself. I was ready. Ready for oblivion.

I let go of the railing, falling forward with a smile on my lips, eyes closed and arms stretched out wide. I could feel my feet leave the edge of the bridge with ease. Wind hit my face and my hair whipped my cheeks, but suddenly, I was moving in the wrong direction. A weight slammed into me, and something tightened around my waist, wrenching me backwards.

I yelped as the breath rushed from my lungs. When my eyes flew open in shock, I watched the ocean fall away as I was moved back over the railing. Arms wrapped around my torso, dragging me backwards as I struggled. I fought them, jerking my body from side to side. The rain was pouring so hard, I could no longer see through it. I struggled so hard that I heard muttering and curses when I hit or kicked or snarled. But in what felt like both seconds and hours at the same time, my world went dark. The scent of burlap overwhelmed my senses. My hands were wrenched behind my back. Someone dragged me backwards, and I let myself become dead weight.

I tried. I tried so hard to fight it. I wanted to go back to that sweet, sweet oblivion waiting for me at the bottom of the harbor. But instead, all that awaited me was the cold metal floor of some kind of large vehicle and the click and clank of heavy locks falling into place as we sped off into the night.

CHAPTER 7
SERENITY

*W*hen I woke up, I was freezing. So cold, my skin ached as I uncurled my limbs. Mouth feeling like cotton and eyes burning as if someone had scrubbed them with sandpaper, I fumbled to sit up before quickly realizing my hands were bound.

Fumbling to my knees, I tried to yank my hands apart, but they caught on a bit of chain between them, connecting the leather cuffs around my wrists. Holy shit...this was bad. This was so fucking bad. My heart started racing, and I willed myself to take in steady, slow breaths. If I passed out again, it wouldn't do me any good.

Just focus... Focus on what you can see. What can you feel? Cold. I could feel cold, an aching, stark cold so deep, my bones throbbed.

It took a moment for my eyes to adjust, and I had to wipe the tears off on my wrists just below the leather cuffs. Whatever room I'd found myself in was nearly pitch black, and the floor beneath my knees was cushioned like a mattress. A blinking red light flashed about ten feet in front of me, and a double image of that little speck glared off of a pane of glass. As my eyes adjusted even more, I realized the room was barren, save for a single rectangular window on the wall in front of me.

"Hello!" I called out, voice croaking as I descended into a coughing fit. For a moment, my eyes blurred and I nearly teetered to the side. My stomach churned. "I said, hello!" I called out again, louder this time.

Met with nothing but silence, I strained to hear through the eerie darkness. I cursed myself now more than ever for neglecting my need for blood. Right now, I wished I was stronger, my senses sharper. I was as pathetic and fragile as a human, and I was paying the price. Watching that red light blink, I counted the seconds between each one. Two seconds, then a blink. Steady. Controlled. I stared at that light and wondered...

Dread churned in my gut as I realized I was being watched. I knew without a doubt that somebody was watching me, probably from the other side of that dark pane of glass. My mind instantly flashed to Carson's dinner party. Memories came flooding back, and fear spiked.

"Carson!" I yelled, pulling my chains tighter. I kicked out, trying to stand, but realized my feet were also in chains, only they were chained to the floor rather than to each other.

It had to be Carson. I remembered the sick gleam in his eyes as his colleagues looked me over, as if I was some sort of commodity. The memory of hands on my skin made bile rise to my throat, but I choked it down. I needed to focus. I needed to get my head on straight and think of a way out of this. The first thing I had to do was figure out who really had me here. The list of suspects was a long one. I was Ryan Harker's daughter, and his enemies were numerous.

But Carson... I could try and explain away his cold ruth-lessness as a product of both of our fathers and the stark-ness of the reality we lived in, where hatred bred wars that could never be won, not for either side. I could come up with lists of excuses for him, but in the end, I knew the truth. He, like my father and many other men leading this fight against the darklings, was a monster. They were all the real monsters, simply hiding behind human flesh and bone.

I nearly yelped when the lights flipped on. The room was bathed in red, illuminating a twenty by twenty space. The walls were covered floor to ceiling in black, tufted padding. Red lamps swung overhead, and I blinked against the harshness. There was indeed a window in front of me, but it was still tinted too dark to see through, even as I strained and squinted. That red light on the other side was still blinking. I yanked against the chains that held my hands together and searched for a way free, but it was useless. My ankles were in chains, and those chains were bolted to the tufted padding, under which they were prob-ably anchored in place by a slab of concrete.

The room was silent one moment, until a faint buzzing filled the space. It was quiet, and if I'd been fully human, I probably wouldn't have even picked up on the change. I heard rustling, something like the swish of clothing or the brush of footsteps over carpet. Instinctively, I looked to the mirror once again, eyes widening as I beheld a small red room on the other side. It was as if someone had pressed a button and the mirror had become a window.

My heart raced as I stared at the three figures on the other side of that window. They were clad in dark hoodies pulled up over their heads and stared back at me from behind masks made of mirrors. No features. No holes for eyes or a mouth. Nothing but three mirrored surfaces looking out at me as if in pity. I could see a faint image of myself in the mirrors, even from here. My pale pink dress hung in tatters, practically nonexistent, leaving me clad in my black bralette, lace panties, and matching garter set. My stockings were torn away, and the room grew colder. They were tall, I could tell. Broad shouldered and sturdy. Men, I concluded, remembering the heavy hands that had grabbed me before shoving me in that van.

"Carson?" I choked, barely containing a gag. Fear curled in my stomach, my brain flipping through the thousands of possible scenarios these insane men had in store for me. "Carson, please...just let me out. We can forget—"

Deep, rumbling laughter cut off my useless plea. Chills climbed my arms and legs. "You call out for a man who would sell you as a broodmare," the voice said. I watched with wide eyes as one of the masked men took a step forward.

The deepness of the voice was obviously artificial. It was as if he were speaking into a talk box, disguising his voice from me. Still, it only served to make me shake. I cursed myself for being so fucking weak. Had it really come to this?

"Tell me, Miss Harker, what is it you think you're doing here?" he asked.

His question threw me, and I stuttered, "I-I don't know what you mean." Tears stung my eyes, but I blinked them away. One single tear, and they'd know what I was. If this wasn't Cason, then I couldn't take that chance.

"You're here because your father has been very, very naughty," he said with a chuckle, that voice box crackling. "You're here because you have information we seek."

I shook my head, mouth opening and closing as his words sunk in. I had no idea what he was talking about. What information? I didn't know a thing. I was a trophy, an ornament. What the fuck did I have to do with my father?

"I swear I don't know anything. Whatever he's done, I promise I had noth—"

"I don't believe I asked you to speak again."

One of the men turned and stalked off to the side, and then I heard the opening and shutting of a door. The lights went out, and I was bathed in a sudden darkness that my eyes couldn't adjust to fast enough. It was mere seconds before they flickered back on again, and a scream tore from my throat. He was standing in front of me, inches away, as I knelt at his feet. Heavy black boots, dark pants, black hoodie with the hood pulled up over that mirrored mask. He was even larger than he'd looked through that window, and he had his arms crossed over his chest. I tried to back up, but the chains pulled taut. The other two simply watched, those masks hiding any sort of emotion completely.

The man knelt until he was sitting in a squat position, elbows placed over his knees. The position brought our faces close together, but still I couldn't see past the mirrored surface. I could only see my own reflection on it—pale hair in a disarray, skin ashy and bloodless, and my brown eyes reddened and wide and full of dread.

"What do you want from me?" I whispered, eyes boring into the space where his should be, hoping he could understand that I truly did know nothing. "Whatever you want to know about Ryan Harker, I don't have the answer. You're asking the wrong person..."

Silence met my plea. The man raised a leather glove clad hand, reaching towards my face. I flinched away instinctively. That hand stopped before touching my skin, giving me enough time to recover and glance back up. I stopped breathing as the tips of his fingers met my hairline.

The feel of the expensive leather had tingles and heat spreading through my body. It was a soft touch, and wholly unexpected. I wished I could see through to the face behind the mask. Eyes were a window to the soul and all that.

In a blink, those caressing fingers moved, faster than I could have anticipated, and gripped my chin. He forced me to face the window, towards the other two, who looked on as if expecting this. My chin pulsed with bruising pain where his fingers squeezed, but I didn't tear my eyes from that window.

He faced the window, too. "Tell me this pretty head wouldn't look lovely spiked on the gates of city hall," the man said, and my breath stalled. Up close, his voice was as deep as thunder and ripped through the room like a storm, his words sending fear skittering through my bones. "You know what we want, and you have forty-eight hours to respond, Senator."

Once more, my eyes caught on that blinking red light. There, in the center of that room, placed between the two remaining men, was a camera, small, black, and blinking. My breath caught as a cold sliver of metal pressed against my throat. I was afraid to swallow against the knife I knew the man had placed against my throat, his other hand still holding my chin in place.

I stared at that blinking light, wondering if the feed was live. I wondered who was watching right now. Was it Carson? Was it Ryan? Both? What about my mother? Could she see me kneeling here at the mercy of these strange men? But worst of all, would she care?

I wanted to open my mouth. I wanted to plead with my father to comply with their demands...whoever they were. But I knew it was hopeless. Ryan Harker wasn't my father. He had no obligation to barter for my freedom. There was nothing he needed from me, and if anything, it would only bolster support from the rest of his fanatical disciples. He'd find some way to spin this kidnapping to benefit him. Whoever these men were, they clearly had no idea who they were dealing with.

I looked up at the man who held my face, the light in my eyes dying in my reflection as he whispered, "You're not safe anymore. I promise you that."

Safe... I didn't know the meaning of the word.

I didn't know how long I'd been lying here after the men left. There were no windows, no clock, no hourly visits. Nothing with which to gauge the hours or days as they passed. I drifted in and out of sleep.

A few hours ago—or I supposed it could have been any amount of time—a woman had bustled in, dropping a plate of food only feet away from where I curled up on the floor. I only knew she was a woman because of the faint floral smell of her and the lightness of her steps. I hadn't seen her before she was out of the room again, bathing me once more in darkness. I'd eaten the delicious steak they'd given me, savoring the perfect juiciness of the meat. I was so hungry, I didn't even care if it was poisoned.

It surprised me, the fact that they'd given me such exquisite food and thick red wine to wash it down with. I guzzled that, letting it drip down the sides of my face as I moaned at the rich flavor. When I was finished, I'd taken to pacing, though I couldn't go far. The chains pulled tight seven feet from the center of the room. I screamed a few times. I cursed those hooded men and raged, slinging every insult I could think of towards that fucking window. I glared at the little red dot the whole time.

I refused to shed a single tear. I was done crying. If this was the way I was supposed to die, then so be it. I'd been ready to leap to my death on that bridge. Actually...I *had* leapt to my death, and I would have succeeded if it hadn't been for this unwanted intervention. I wanted to do it again. I wanted to end it, to slit my wrists and watch the blood drain from my veins as I slowly fell into a deep sleep. Or perhaps I could force these men to kill me somehow. Make it quick. I wanted this to end.

After counting four unrestful sleeps that could have been naps for all I knew, I saw the red lights flicker on behind my lids. I tried to sit up and catch them entering the room, but I was too slow. A small gust of smoke scented air wafted over my face, and in less than a heartbeat, one of the masked men was standing before me. I ran my eyes up the length of him, from his heavy boots to the dark clothing and gloves. I swore I could still feel the brush of that leather over my face. I looked even worse than before as I gazed at my reflection in the mask. Remnants of that delicious red wine left red tracks down the edges of my mouth, running down my neck, and I could have sworn the man was looking at them.

His hands balled into fists, and I could hear the squeak and brush of the leather as it moved. I fought the urge to fidget as he said, "Up." It was a command. No room for argument.

I didn't move. I just sat there as he waited, and it didn't even look like he was breathing. Fuck this guy and his orders. Fuck him for keeping me here like an animal. Men were all the same, just different breeds of them. The fact that he wasn't working with Ryan Harker should have made me feel some small sliver of comfort, but I was beginning to feel the opposite. There was something sinister about the aura around this man. Something heavy and dark hovered around him, and it was like my body screamed that he wasn't human.

I kept my face stone still as he crouched into a squat. For the life of me, I couldn't even tell if this was the same man as before. With those hoodies and masks covering every inch of skin, there was no way for me to tell them apart. Reaching down, he now wielded a key and proceeded to unlock the chains that bound my feet to the floor. The very second they were free, I kicked out as hard as I could manage, hitting him square in the gut.

He didn't budge an inch. I might not be strong in vampire terms, but I wasn't human. That kick should have toppled him, as I'd used every single ounce of my strength. He was as still as a statue as I fell backwards, leg throbbing from the impact. He sighed audibly, as if he was dealing with some kind of petulant child and not a captive woman. Reaching for me, he sighed again as I used both forearms to smack his hand away.

I knew I couldn't keep this up. I knew he could over-power me if he wanted to, and he proved that in the next second as he grabbed me by the shoulders and hauled me to my feet. The pressure of his fingers on my skin was like a vice.

"Let me go, you fucking bastard!" I spat. Wiggling, I tried to make it as difficult as possible for him to maneuver me.

He ignored me, spinning me around in his strong arms and pulling me against his chest. I was about to say some-thing else when my vision went dark again, and I felt some-thing like cloth covering my eyes. Clamping my mouth tight, I let him walk me forward, knowing I'd probably end up getting hurt if I fought him. I'd never felt his sort of raw strength before. He had to be a vampire or maybe a wolf, but he wasn't human.

I'd have to wait for the right moment to make my move next time. I couldn't be so reckless. They obviously needed me for something. They thought I had some sort of information they needed against Ryan, but soon, they'd realize how much I really didn't know and find other uses for me. I knew how this shit worked, and I knew my time was running out.

I nearly stumbled as my feet left the cushioned floor, hitting cold tile. Remarkably, I was able to stay balanced as the man's hands pushed me onward. I could have fought harder, but I wanted to get some more information. We walked for what felt like no more than a minute, until suddenly, the temperature of the room changed drastically. Where it was once frigid and cold, steam hit my face and the air grew thick with moisture.

The tile under my feet felt slick, and the man pulled on my shoulders, forcing me to stop. I listened without question, but kept my ears open and my nose exploring as I sniffed deeply. Something floral hung in the air. Not the same smell that hovered around the woman who brought me food earlier, but something pungent and thick. Running water hit the hard floor somewhere close by, and immediately, I realized where I was.

I heard a door shut and multiple locks slide into place before the covering was ripped from my eyes. Bright white light blinded me, and I shied away from it, bringing my bound hands up to cover up my eyes. The man walked around me, and I heard his footsteps slapping against the tile. Slowly, I blinked against the light, allowing my hands to fall as I inspected the room.

I was right in thinking I was in a bathroom. The water, the moisture in the air, and the oppressive heat was nearly stifling. The room was made of pristine white marble tiles, and the floor sloped ever so slightly downwards towards a small drain in the center. Multiple showerheads lined the walls, but it wasn't dingy like I'd expected. In fact, the entire room seemed sterile.

I watched the hooded man rip off a glove, revealing pale skin and masculine fingers. He dipped his hand into the shower spray before pulling back and wicking the water off, testing the water, I supposed. I just watched him as he pulled the other glove off, setting them both aside meticulously along a small stainless steel basin.

"Strip," he ordered. Once again, that artificial voice made my heart dip as it echoed in the acoustics of the bathroom. When I made no move to comply, he took a single step forward. "You either take your clothes off on your own, or I will tie you to a wall and cut them off with my knife. Your choice."

My jaw clenched, and I bit back a *fuck you*. I needed to tread lightly, so I just said, "Kind of hard to do that with my hands tied up." Holding up my hands, I stared at the man dubiously.

It was infuriating not being able to see his expression behind the mirror, but mentally, I pictured him rolling his eyes. He strode towards me, and it took every effort not to back away. Instead, I squared my shoulders until we were toe to toe.

He ducked down slightly, bringing his mask close enough to touch the tip of my nose. "If you try anything stupid, I'll find far more interesting things to do with said knife. Make one wrong move, and you'll regret it. Do you understand?"

I didn't answer. I just met his stare. Or I assumed I did.

"Do. You. Understand." It was a statement now, not a question. Even through the voice box, I could hear the irritation, like a coil about to snap.

Instead of answering verbally, I gave him a single curt nod, to which he must have found acceptable because he straightened up and pulled out a key, which he used to unlock the cuffs, freeing my hands. He let them fall to the floor before backing away until he was leaning against the metal basin. I watched him fold his arms over his chest, muscles flexing, even under the black hoodie. He was a massive man, I could tell. His waist tapered into a hard, narrow V, and his stance was wide. Seven foot, I suspected. I was an ant in comparison. A child.

I looked him up and down blatantly and gave him a mean smirk. "You're wasting both my time and yours, buddy. You want something from me that I simply don't have for you. Why don't you just speed this along and kill me now?"

He was silent for a minute, and I thought he wouldn't respond to my goading, until he said, "And that's what you want, isn't it? To die?" His voice was sharp, but inquisitive. "That's why you leapt from that bridge like a coward."

"You don't know anything about me," I gritted out through my teeth. "You saw one single moment in my life where I made the best decision I could, but don't you ever presume to know anything about my motivations."

"Death is the easy way out—"

"Death is nothing!" I snapped, barely letting him finish his sentence. I looked him straight in the mask without blinking. "Death is the only way to achieve nothing."

He didn't respond. I didn't think he was going to anytime soon, so I turned away. Stepping farther into the room, I spotted a hook on the far wall and headed for it, grabbing the straps of my ruined dress. I tore the offensive pink garment off, letting it all to the floor. I took more care with my bralette and panties, stripping them off fluidly, uncaring of the man standing against the far wall watching my every move. I didn't care what he saw.

When I was naked, I made for the shower head, delighting in the luxurious feel of warm water hitting my face as I got closer. When I was fully beneath the spray, I tilted my head back, letting the heat cascade over my face, and moaned. A shiver rolled through my body. I hadn't realized how cold I'd been earlier, and the thought of going back into that padded room had dread pooling in my gut.

On the wall were soap dispensers, each labeled with shampoo, conditioner, and body wash, so I used each one in order. The soaps smelled of lilac and roses, and I used them to scrub vigorously until I thought my skin might start bleeding. I didn't know what I was trying to wash away—the nightmarish feel of lecherous eyes crawling over my skin, or the weakness I could still feel clinging to me like a blanket of shame.

I could feel the man watching me, could feel the heat of his gaze as if he was touching my body, and I hated myself for the pleasure the thought brought me. What kind of sick bitch did that make me? After all I'd been through in the last...day...two days? No way to know, but after all I'd been through, you'd think I'd shy away from it.

I scrubbed the conditioner out of my long white blonde hair, sifting the pearly strands through my fingers. I reveled in the feel of the floral smelling steam, wondering how long it would be until I was allowed another shower. I was surprised they were even allowing me this.

The man watched me in silence, and I wondered just how many of my scars he was able to make out through the thick steam. I knew my back was littered with them. They'd heal one day, if I ever decided to give into the bloodlust. When I relinquished the hold my mortality had on me, I could rid myself of the memory of each blow, kick and cut. But for now, they decorated my skin like a brand, marking me as a coward.

The water shut off on its own, and I heard heavy steps behind me. My body went still, muscles tensing up, afraid to turn around or look over my shoulder. I felt a presence behind me and knew the man was there, waiting for me to acknowledge him. So I did. I turned in place, craning my neck as I looked up and up and up, meeting that mirrored stare. I should have felt uncomfortable with him standing in my personal space, especially given the fact that I was naked, wet, and vulnerable. I should have taken a step away or covered myself, but I had no such inclination.

Despite the scare tactics and the voicebox, I didn't feel like this man was sadistic. Though he exuded a dark aura of danger unlike anything I'd ever experienced, I didn't get the feeling that he wanted me to suffer. Not like Carson. There had been times in the past where Carson's mere touch had made me recoil, as if my body's fight or flight was kicking in without me realizing it. I knew what evil felt like. This wasn't it.

It took a second to realize the man was holding a towel. I stared at it for a heartbeat before taking it and wrapping it around myself. He watched me the whole time. I watched him back though, closely. Fuck, he was large. Strong too. There was no way I'd be able to fight him off and escape. Trying would be stupid and reckless.

"We've provided you a change of clothes," he spoke suddenly. "Dress yourself."

I followed his gesture to the hook and realized my

clothes were no longer hanging there. Frowning, I spied another garment in their place. I looked at the man in question. "Where are my clothes?"

"None of your concern. Get dressed before I run out of patience."

"And what will you do then, big man?" I sneered, unable to help myself.

He took a menacing step towards me. "I can always drag you back naked."

"Fuck you," I spat.

"I can do that too." It was casual, the way he said it. A threat and a promise.

I stomped over to the hook and made quick work of drying myself off. I tried to ignore the tingle of awareness that plagued my traitorous body. His offer still rolled around in my head, causing my thighs to clench. I hated myself for it. For the life of me, I couldn't wipe the sudden image of the man pounding into me against the wall out of my head. I pictured those leather gloves running over my clit. I pictured those massive hands holding me aloft as I screamed out in pleasure. My pussy throbbed, and I wanted to die right there.

I was about to reach for the garment on the hook when a soft gust of air rolled over my naked flesh. The smell of leather surrounded me, and I froze. I could barely breathe, because I knew he was right there, right over my shoulder. The slightest touch almost had me leaping out of my skin. Leather again, so he must have put his gloves back on. A thrill ran through me, much to my own dismay. I could feel him at my back, the fabric of his shirt brushing my spine. He was so large, I knew he could peer straight down over my shoulders.

"I can smell what you'd like me to do to you," he whispered. The talk box had his voice coming out more like an animalistic growl. "You're pussy is wet right now, isn't it, Serenity?"

My name on his lips had me squirming as my nipples pebbled. I tried to fight it off. I didn't want to feel this way. It was wrong, and I knew it. I should have been disgusted, but I wasn't. I wanted more of those whispers. Some deep, dark part of my soul was opening up, craving the barely restrained violence and promise I could feel emanating from the masked man.

I found myself saying, "Get away from me." Though I knew I didn't mean it.

I think he could tell, because he chuckled. The sound was terrifying and dark. "Are you afraid?" he asked, and I stiffened some more as his gloved fingertips grazed my hip. "Fear only heightens the senses. Makes every touch all the more exquisite."

I was holding my breath, letting his hand snake over my bare skin until he reached the apex of my thighs. I should have been stopping this. This was so fucking wrong on so many levels. But my clit throbbed, my thighs begged to rub together, and my skin was feverish.

"Don't move an inch," he said darkly. "You move and this stops. You stay still, and I'll make you feel something."

"Why?" I whispered, unable to help myself.

He chuckled again before saying, "Because I'm not a good man, Serenity."

Leather grazed my clit, and my legs nearly buckled. The pad of a single gloved finger pressed down, applying pressure, and I wanted to scream. He began swirling that finger around the little bundle of nerves, but it was slow at first, just a tease. It was torture trying not to grind against him.

Lips pressed together to keep from moaning, I focused all my energy on remaining in a standing position.

He added another finger, swirling them in lightning fast movements. I was so wet, I could hear the gloves slicking off of me. The leather was soft and luxurious, and the texture only heightened every sensation. My legs parted as I tipped my head back, trying to keep the tears at bay. It felt so good, I was shaking. I knew I was close. I needed to come so badly, I could burst. Then his fingers dipped inside me, and the heel of his palm slapped against my clit as he fucked me hard and fast with his fingers.

I could no longer hold in the scream. It ripped from my lips as I fell back against his massive chest, and my pussy clamped around his fingers hard as I came. Lights exploded in my vision. He kept moving but slowed down gradually, and every swipe of his palm had my knees begging to give out. I'd never felt anything like it before, but once I let myself calm down a little, the shame started to roll in.

He must have noticed the difference because he pulled his fingers out and backed away. I rocked forward, catching myself on the tile wall, and tried to regulate my breathing. The man was just standing there, watching me, and I was terrified and ashamed of turning around, only to see nothing but my own disgusting reflection staring back at me.

So I ignored him. I just grabbed for the black silk garment hanging from the hook. It was a lightweight nightie and I internally rolled my eyes, but I slipped it on, suddenly grateful to be covered up.

"That was a one time thing," I muttered without turning around.

Silence. He said absolutely nothing, and it made my teeth grind.

Breathing in deeply, I gathered the strength to square my shoulders and turn around to face him. He was still just standing there, hands at his sides, fingers slick with my wetness. Right then, I swore I would give anything to see behind that mask. I wanted to see the expression on his face. I wanted to read his eyes. But there was nothing, just a mirror. We stared at each other for too long to be comfortable, and eventually, he was the one to break the moment.

Reaching behind him, the man pulled out the leather cuffs again and held them taut. My belly flipped, this time with nausea at the thought of returning to that room, that padded cell. I let him cuff me and then blindfold me shortly after.

"Why are you doing this to me?" I asked. "I meant it when I said I didn't have the information you need. Ryan Harker doesn't tell me anything. If he did something fucked up, which I'm sure he did, then I'm sorry, but it has nothing to do with me."

The man didn't speak. He didn't make any indication he'd heard me at all. He simply turned me around and began walking me out. I felt the change in the air again as we made it out of that large bathroom. The cold was even more stark after becoming used to the steamy heat. He led me in silence, not saying a word, and I wondered how long this would go on. How long was I supposed to suffer for Ryan's crimes? When would it end? *How* would it end?

It should've been on my terms. I wished it could've been.

CHAPTER 8
SERENITY

The next day passed in much the same fashion. I spent my time lying on the padded floor, chained there like a dog. My captors must have been watching me closely, because they caught on to my sleeping schedule fast. When I woke up, it was usually to find a fresh plate of food in front of me.

I ate, though reluctantly. They alternated bringing me water and wine. I preferred the wine. As a dhampir, I didn't actually need much food or drink. In the twelve months since that side of me woke up, I'd realized I was changing. I did a lot of research in the days following the assassination of my brother. When the spray of his blood hit my face and a single drop hit my tongue, it'd woken up the creature in me, and then it was all downhill from there.

I'd become stronger at first, before my body realized I was letting it starve. I was faster, sharper, and even a bit smarter. It was like my entire body was functioning at a level of perfection a human could never achieve. I hated the sun, but didn't burn in it like a vampire. Dhampirs were abominations in the human world, but I didn't understand the hatred. Right now though, as I lay on the floor staring at the ceiling, I wondered what would've happened to me had I given into the bloodlust. Would I have been strong enough to stop Carson or Ryan? Would I have been so easily captured by these mysterious men?

I didn't know. The what-ifs were likely going to keep me up at night for the foreseeable future. There were so many things I could've done differently, and I could spend the rest of my life dwelling on them. But then how would that help me? What I needed to do was figure out a way to handle these men. I needed to know what it was they thought I knew. Obviously, there was some kind of secret that they believed Ryan told me, even if they were dead wrong.

Ryan Harker was a lot of things—a horrible man, a sadist, a racist, and a liar. Those were just the names that stuck out the most. Even before we found out I wasn't his, I knew there was something off about him. I still didn't understand the draw my mother must've felt towards him. Sure he was handsome, but it was a plastic sort of charm. None of it was real, and apparently, my mom was too dense to realize that. I wanted to feel bad for her, having to share his bed and smile for his cameras all day, every day. I couldn't imagine she'd planned for her life to end up like this.

But as bad as I felt, I knew she'd made her own bed. She'd married a wealthy and powerful man, and still made the choice to go behind his back with a vampire and have a child. What the hell was she thinking?

The lights went off, and my whole body locked up. A wind rushed through the quiet room, and when it was bathed in red light once more, a man was standing in front of me. He still wore the usual dark hood, thick boots, and the off-putting mirror mask. I hated it. I wanted to rip it off his face and expose the coward underneath. What were they so afraid of? My only hope was the notion that perhaps they planned to eventually release me, and therefore, couldn't risk me seeing their faces. That small sliver of hope was the only thing grounding me right now.

"On your knees," the man ordered. His distorted voice boomed through the room, leaving me no choice but to listen.

I scrambled up onto my knees, hands bound before me as the man knelt down to unlock the chains around my ankles. He grabbed my upper arm and hauled me to my feet. My first instinct was to struggle, but I thought better of it. He was stronger than me. Possibly a vampire, or maybe a shifter. Either way, he wasn't human, and he could probably snap my neck as easily as blinking.

He pushed, causing me to stagger back, nearly toppling over. The room wasn't very large, so in seconds, my back was slamming up against the padding on the wall. He loomed over me like a giant, all bulging muscles that he couldn't hide beneath the hoodie. "Stand still," he said sharply.

I did. I barely moved a muscle on my own as he reached out, lifting my right arm to the side. He released my arm, but it pulled taut. He moved onto the other arm, and in a few swift movements, I was cuffed to little metal loops jutting from the cushioned wall. Next, he moved to my legs, locking them into a wide stance. Panic was slowly creeping up.

"W-What are you doing?" I stammered. "What is this?!"

"Be quiet," he snapped.

"Tell me what's going—"

His hand wrapped around my throat, leather creaking as he added pressure, bringing his face close to mine. I stared into my own reflection as he said, "Not another word. Be silent, or I'll give that mouth something else to do."

My belly flipped as he held me in his grip. I should have been petrified. I should have been thrashing and fighting him off, but all I could do was stare, trying to breathe around the pressure of those thick fingers. Was this the one who made me come in the bathroom? I couldn't tell. If I wasn't mistaken, this one seemed slightly taller than the other one had. I wondered if he knew what his friend had done to me, if it was a part of their diabolical plan. Or perhaps the other one had slipped up and let his lust over-power his hostage taking mindset.

His hands left my throat, and he turned away, facing that massive dark window with the still blinking red light. Realization dawned on me. We must have reached the forty-eight hour mark. Was that all? Time seemed all wrong in here. In a blink, the lights went out again and came back on just as fast. I nearly yelped as the two other men appeared, standing with the third. They moved fast and were silent as the wind.

My heart threatened to crawl into my throat as they stalked closer. Their footsteps didn't make a sound. The dark window flickered for a moment, and I blinked as the image of Ryan Harker appeared before me. The window apparently doubled as a screen, and those watery blue eyes stared back at me without emotion. Two men stood to his side, but their faces were out of frame. I imagined they were my failed bodyguards, and a brand new wave of anger swam through me. They'd done nothing to help me when Carson let those men ogle me. They were supposed to protect me from harm, and yet they'd just stood there.

"Senator Ryan Harker, what is your answer?" one of the men asked, straight to the point, no bullshit.

Ryan took a few heartbeats to answer, but when he did, it left me cold, though I should have expected it. "I'm afraid I cannot help you, gentlemen."

"Lies," one of the men hissed.

Ryan raised a single tawny brow. "My my, how volatile." His thinning lips quirked up on the side before his eyes shifted to meet mine. "How are they treating you, sweetheart? Three square meals a day?"

I bit my tongue against telling him how I really felt. Now wasn't the time. I wanted to know what it was these men needed from him. The fires of hell must have burned in my eyes, because my former father only smiled wider.

"You'll receive nothing from me. Humans do not make deals with our inferiors," Ryan said smugly. "Or is there no honor among monsters that you have to resort to kidnapping to get your point across?"

"You'd risk your flesh and blood?" one of the men with me asked, taking a step forward.

Ryan's grin was becoming sickening as he said, "We all have to make sacrifices for the things we believe in. My lovely Serenity will make a beautiful martyr, will she not?"

I was still staring into his evil eyes as a blackness fell over my vision. This time, I did struggle a bit as a blindfold was pulled tight. My heart leapt into my throat when I felt someone brush my hair from the right side of my neck. Fingers once again wrapped around my throat and squeezed. Fear overcame me, and I struggled, knowing there was nothing I could do to break these cuffs and chains.

"We'll drain the girl dry, Harker," one of the men threatened.

"I call your bluff," Ryan responded.

A burning sensation raced over my skin the moment a set of fangs sunk into my neck. It happened so fast, I didn't have time to brace for it. My whole body went still as the burning tingled. I squirmed, trying to get away, but no matter what I did, nothing happened. The man held my throat tighter as his mouth coaxed blood from my veins. Just as an intense sort of pleasure began to spread from my neck to my limbs, whoever was drinking my blood tore away, and I cried out as their teeth were ripped from my skin. A hot trickle of blood slithered down my skin, and for a moment, it was silent enough to hear the drops hit the floor.

"What is this?!" one of the men shouted, his voice ending on a hiss. Fingers clamped around my throat, cutting off my air as breath fanned over my face. "Dhampir!"

The word penetrated the silence, then I heard the two others curse and stagger backwards. I fought a grin. I couldn't help it. They really hadn't known. This whole time, I'd suspected I'd been found out, and a little part of me even thought that perhaps my lineage was a part of the big secret. But they hadn't known.

"Your daughter is a dhampir," someone said, and was only rewarded with Ryan's low chuckle.

"I'm honestly surprised it took this long for you to work that out. For one of the oldest covens in the world, you're severely lacking in intel."

"Explain," someone hissed. Those fingers were still wrapped around my throat, and I felt the blood draining away and covering his hand. I could still hear the *drip drip drip* onto the floor.

"The beauty of a kidnapping is I don't owe you a damn thing. You kill her, and she'll be a martyr for my cause. The humans will riot in the streets for her safety."

He was right. I knew they would. Tensions were already high out there. Every day, I worried about Trix and her protests. She was a dedicated activist, but I knew the humans had their extremists. If the public knew that the precious, angelic Serenity Harker was being held captive by a vampire coven... Wait a second... Oldest coven in the world? It couldn't be, could it? Atlas. Atlas Nocturne had kidnapped me.

My mind was racing, and I knew the man with his hand around my neck could feel the fresh gush of blood as my heart sped up. I flickered through memories of the other night—the night I'd unwittingly thrown myself right into the coven leader's arms. Of course, I hadn't known it was him, but that whole night, despite Ryan's beating, I'd dreamed of those red vampire eyes. If I thought about it hard enough, I could still feel the pleasurable tingle of his tongue and the silk of his midnight hair as it sifted through my fingers.

My body was utterly still, and I was tuning out the conversation around me. The men were attempting to barter with my life in exchange for some mystery information, and it got me wondering... Were these men simply henchmen, or was Atlas in this room right now? Was he...

Holy shit, the bathroom. Had that been Atlas back there? It had to be. There's no way a henchman for the most notorious vampire coven leader would have taken that kind of risk. Defying a coven leader was as close to treason as you could get as far as I knew. The more I thought about it, the more certain I became. It had to have been him. Why did that notion send a sudden thrill through my entire body?

"Goodnight, gentlemen," I heard Ryan say.

Nobody responded, and shortly after, I heard something metallic bounce off of what sounded like glass, but there was no shatter or crash. I assumed the glass was bulletproof then.

Blackness receded as the blindfold was ripped off my

face. I blinked in the red light, my vision slowly clearing, only to realize the three masked men stood in a line right in front of me. I couldn't help the manic grin that stretched my lips. "Daddy dearest playing hardball, is he?"

The man in the center grabbed my throat again, and a hysterical laugh tumbled from my lips before I could stop myself. His fingers only tightened as I gritted out, "When will you learn that these tactics won't work on me?" I smiled as the pressure lessened. "You need something from me, because clearly Ryan isn't giving it up." I squinted at the men. "You won't kill me just yet."

"When were you going to tell us you're a dhampir?" the one on the left asked.

"Never."

"Why?"

"Frankly, because it's none of your fucking business," I spat out. "Someone should have done their homework."

"Senator Harker knew all this time?"

I snorted. "You think I have these scars because I'm clumsy?"

Silence met my rhetorical question, and I could feel their hidden eyes roving over my exposed skin. In the harsh red light, the small scars that were usually concealed by expertly placed makeup or clothing were glaring and had a slight silvery sheen. I could feel judgement in those stares, and I didn't like it.

"Is Senator Harker your biological father?"

"No."

Silence. I'd told them the truth. There was nothing they could do realistically. If they killed me, at least I could die without having to do the hard part myself. But if they let me go, there was a possibility that I could fake my death and leave the city without Ryan or Carson ever knowing. I didn't want to give that fantasy too much thought, because even I could tell how far-fetched it was.

I stood there, chained against the wall, staring at my kidnappers. I was waiting for them to come to a decision, but from the looks of things, they were just as confused as I was. The one on the right was repeatedly balling and flexing his fingers, while the other two stood stock still.

"I'm not sure what the hell you people even want, and I can promise you chances are, I don't know a thing, but this isn't how you're going to get answers."

They still said nothing. They just stared at me for what felt like a lifetime as my wrists and ankles began to grow numb. I was done talking. They could either do this the civilized way, or they could kill me and end this torture once and for all. My eyes were beginning to lose focus as the lights once again shut off, and with a rush of wind, I knew the men were gone.

CHAPTER 9
MERRICK

$\mathcal{I}$ walked alongside Senator Ryan Harker, eyes on a swivel. He and his entourage descended the steps of the capitol building, where a host of reporters crushed together, cameras already flashing.

I'd kept an eye on the senator inside the building, taking note of the micro expressions others might not pick up on. I tracked the cadence of his voice as he conversed with members of the senate or emissaries from other districts. Sol District's matron, Estelle Nightingale, had been present in negotiations today, and I hadn't missed the disgust present in Harker's eyes as he pretended to be polite. He was all smiles for the witch, eyes twinkling on the surface, but I'd had a chance to see beneath it.

When I thought of that night at Carson Badgeley's estate, it made my teeth grind. Every moment since the senator's daughter had fled the estate, I'd been fighting a battle between keeping up this charade and grinding Carson's bones to dust. It wasn't easy, but there were bigger things going on. I needed to play this right if we had even a sliver of a chance at finding the prisons.

For nearly ten years now, we'd been hunting the location of four holding facilities created by the human factions and their donors. The human districts were growing denser and more radical every year. At first, it was simply a few religious zealots claiming the darklings were demons here to wipe humanity from the earth. We'd dismissed the threat too easily, because within a decade, their rhetoric spread, and soon, men like Senator Harker rose to power and threw fuel on that fire.

Darkling women had been going missing. It seemed there were at least two every month who never returned home. The human police were no help and shrugged the disappearances off as flighty darklings who decided to leave the city. They didn't give a shit about the pattern of disappearances and how abruptly they'd sprung up.

Inside intelligence told us these women had been targeted specifically. Usually half-blooded darklings between the ages of seventeen and twenty-eight, or at least their presenting age. The races varied, but they were mostly half-bloods. The latest in the string of disappearances happened to be a woman by the name of Loxley Nocturne, Atlas Nocturne's half-sister. They'd made a mistake in that particular selection, as Atlas already had a bone to pick with the human senator said to be responsible for the disappearances.

I stood behind Harker as he smiled and waved for the cameras. He appeared unruffled, polished, and charming to the masses. I'd never understood how humans could be so fickle. The sun glared down on us, winking off the white marble steps of the historical building, and my eyes burned, even behind these dark shades. The potion was beginning to wane, and I knew I needed to swig some more before the day was through. I glanced to my right and knew Faust was already looking at me. Small beads of sweat trickled down his neck, and he shuffled from foot to foot, grinding his teeth. Bastian's potion was potent, tasted like garbage, and made me vomit every time, but I was thankful for it. Otherwise, we wouldn't have been able to keep this game going. But if the senator took any fucking longer to please his disciples, there was a very real chance our skin might start to smoke.

Sometimes, I found myself missing the sun. What I could remember of it, anyway. When I was human, I'd lived in Ireland. Back then, before technology, before nuclear war or smog or all the shit that came with modern society, I'd been at peace. I'd had a good wife, two small boys, and a modest home in the village my family had founded centuries before. Sometimes, that life seemed so far away, I wondered if it wasn't simply a fever dream. It was growing harder and harder to picture Siobhan's face...

I shook off the memories as a commotion headed for the steps. People were shoving at each other, everyone clamouring to view the massive screen perched in the city center. What used to be a billboard advertisement for the upcoming election was now an image of a woman, blindfolded and chained against a dark padded wall. She wore a black night dress and her white blonde hair was in a disarray around her shoulders, falling nearly to her waist.

The crowd went utterly still and silent, and it even took a moment for Senator Harker to catch onto what had pulled their attention away from him. I watched along with everyone else, and for a moment, my heart lurched. Its nearly nonexistent beat was already sluggish, but staring at the woman bound in cuffs with all that milky skin on display had my cock thickening in my pressed slacks.

She looked delectable in those bindings, and my mouth began to water. My eyes flitted to Faust, only to find him utterly stone still, also staring at the screen. There was just something about the famous Serenity Harker that made my dick hard. From the second I saw her that morning standing in her kitchen wearing nothing but a long shirt, I knew I wanted to fuck her. I'd seen her on TV many times over the years and always knew she was a gorgeous woman. That long white hair was like liquid moonlight against her porcelain skin. It contrasted so beautifully with those chocolate eyes and thick red lips.

She was the Angel of Noc City. Beloved by the humanas who worshiped her father. But there she was, chained to a wall, nipples hard and poking against the silk of her black nightgown. Those red lips stood in stark contrast to the black cloth around her eyes. Blood leaked from the side of her neck, trailing in red rivers over her skin before dripping to the floor.

It took seconds for the crowd to erupt into a frenzy. One moment, it was dead silence, and the next, it was like a wave of chaos swept through the town square. Humans raged, shouting all kinds of slurs and profanities, and some began barreling over the paparazzi, prompting security to come out of the woodwork. I glanced at Faust. This was our cue. We needed to act the part of the vigilant bodyguards and protect the worthless sack of shit gaping at the screen.

Senator Harker blinked away the shock. His acting was fucking impeccable. He looked downright aghast and began shouting something to his PA, who scrambled for her cell phone next to him. Serenity's mother had fainted, and it was only now that I even remembered she was here. The quiet woman was always on the sidelines, trying not to be seen and drunk most of the time.

I whipped out my handgun and circled the senator, taking the steps carefully. Faust and I elbowed people out of the way as they grew irate, shouting at the senator for answers. Answers to why his beloved daughter was tied up and bleeding for all to watch. They demanded to know where she was and who was responsible for this. The crowd was growing by the second as people off the streets looked up at the sound of the yelling and noticed the billboard screen for themselves.

The paparazzi—the ones who'd recovered—were snapping away, making sure to capture every single moment in real time. The senator looked pale, but it only fed into the lie he was suddenly trying to sell. He went to the podium and tapped on the mic, the feedback an ear splitting whine through the eruption of noise, but before he could speak, there was a break in the crowd. I watched helplessly with wide eyes and dread in my gut as two men were dragged forward by a mob of angry human men. I didn't recognize them, but scenting the air, it was clear they were shifters. They were still pups from the looks of it, no more than teenagers, and they were manhandled by the mob of angry humans, who forced them to their knees in front of the steps.

Humans were screaming and cursing the darklings, calling for their immediate extermination. One glance at Faust, and I could tell he was itching to intervene. He met my stare, and I shook my head only a fraction. He had to keep quiet. There was much more riding on this than just these two wolves. Still, the sight of them on their knees, utterly helpless, tore at something inside me. More than that, I was furious. It would be so fucking easy to rip Harker's head from his shoulders. I could do it within seconds, faster than it would take anyone to realize what was happening.

But I couldn't do it yet. We needed him. He had information on the missing half-bloods. He knew where Atlas' sister was, and we couldn't risk her, if she was still alive. Senator Harker was attempting to grab everyone's attention, but the crowd was too hyped up. Too thirsty for darkling blood, so to speak. Once more, I simply watched with my stomach in my throat. I watched and listened as two loud blasts echoed through the town square, then cheers rose up from the crowd of feral humans. I couldn't even close my eyes or look away. They deserved more respect than that. But it only served to fuel my determination to see this through to the end, no matter the cost.

The wolf pups fell dead, bullet holes straight through their foreheads.

CHAPTER 10
SERENITY

"Just tell me what you need to know," I said breathlessly. "It's what you brought me here for, right?" I was still tied to the wall hours later.

I must've fallen asleep at some point, because when I came to, one of the hooded men was standing in the center of the room, staring at me with his arms crossed over his chest. I wondered how long he'd been here, watching me sleep. Once again, I marveled at the size of him. He was all broad shoulders, wide stance, and thick arms.

"You realize I have every reason to despise that man, right?" I gave the man a dubious stare. "Probably even more than you do…"

He loosed something that sounded like a huff or a snort, shaking his head. I felt a sliver of satisfaction that I'd even been able to coax a small reaction from him at all. Surprising me, he said, "I highly doubt that, Miss Harker."

I chuckled darkly. "Miss Harker? A bit formal for a hostage situation, don't you think?"

His shoulders dropped ever so slightly, and I imagined

he was grinning under that mask. I was pushing my luck with these guys, but the longer they held me here, the more I thought about it objectively. I truly didn't think they wanted to cause me real pain for the sake of pain itself. They needed me for something and were simply using the most efficient way of going about achieving it.

"Ryan Harker has something of mine, and I want it back," the man said finally.

Okay...I was not expecting that. "What does he have?" I asked.

"Doesn't matter right now."

"I think it does," I snapped, suddenly even more irritated than before. "You kidnapped me, tied me up like an animal, and drank my blood without my consent. You don't think I at least deserve to know why? You know my biggest secret. I think I'm entitled to something."

The man came closer, taking slow, deliberate steps. I felt my stomach tighten as he came within touching distance, looming over me like a shadow. I could see my angry brown eyes in the reflection of the mirror mask. I looked paler than ever, and there were dark circles under my eyes—a product of the blood loss, no doubt.

"Tell me, Miss Harker..." He came closer, uncomfortably so. I wondered if he could hear my heart racing. Taking a gloved finger, he ran it down the side of my face, trailing it downward towards my collar bone. "Has the bloodlust started yet?" My breath caught as he clicked his tongue. "The cravings can be...intense, to put it mildly."

Turning my face away, I clamped my mouth shut. At the mention of bloodlust, I could feel a stinging in my gums, reminding me of the last time I nearly lost control. I remembered the wild feeling of desperation in that crowd at Rue. I remembered my eyes in that mirror, glossing over in black and red, tiny spidery veins snaking through my skin. I was a monster. Unhinged. Thirsty.

"There she is..." His thumb brushed my throat, and he laid his palm on the side of my neck. I gulped hard as he brought his face closer. "Have you ever indulged, Serenity?" He said my name like he knew me, and I swear my pussy throbbed. My fangs were fully extended now. "No, you wouldn't have, would you? Not the Angel of Noc City."

"Get your hands off of me," I gritted out, trying to keep my fangs concealed. Despite my paleness, I knew my cheeks were turning scarlett. I wasn't embarrassed, per se. I was ashamed. The power his words had over my body made me sick.

"Why don't you tell me what you really want, little dhampir?" he cooed, and the voice box crackled, sending a thrill through my body. "Did you know dhampirs can survive off the blood of both humans and vampires?"

My heart gave a painful lurch. No, I hadn't known that. Why would I?

I could imagine he was grinning under the mask now, knowing he had my attention. He backed away slightly, but instead of leaving, he made a show of slowly pulling off his gloves. Strong pale hands were revealed, each finger holding a different ring with weird, unfamiliar symbols etched into them. I recognized only one, though I'm sure the thought didn't cross his mind. I stared at the symbol of the Nocturne Coven on his middle finger. It was the shape of an upside down cross with a snake coiled up the center. I was right. I knew exactly who my captor was.

I watched in fascination as he transformed his pointer finger into a claw. His nail lengthened to a lethal point, and he brought it to the opposite wrist.

"They say a dhampir's first taste of vampire blood is

sweeter than ambrosia. They say it's better than the best fuck you'll ever have and then some." I could feel that stare down to my bones as he added, "Care to test that theory?"

Holy shit... I couldn't believe he'd just said that. I wished he hadn't, because suddenly, my mouth filled with saliva. I felt my fangs throb, and I knew my eyes were blood red, the monster inside me waking up. She stared at the man who dragged that claw over his pale wrist like he was the juiciest steak she'd ever seen. My pussy throbbed along with my fangs. I wasn't sure how blood and sex were linked exactly, but without a doubt, I knew I wanted to fuck this man while I drained him dry.

It was all wrong in so many ways to want him. He was my captor and I was a hostage. I should be terrified of him and disgusted with myself, but I just couldn't find it in me to care. Something was happening to me. I was turning into a creature who thirsted and hungered and craved. I watched the thin line of blood appear on his wrist and licked my lips. I couldn't tear my eyes away.

"I can feel how much you want it," he purred, slowly lifting his wrist to my face. "You need it, Serenity. You need to drink, or you'll fade away."

I blinked at him, momentarily coming out of my brain fog. "What do you mean I'll fade away?"

"Somehow, your vampire side has woken up. You must have tasted blood at some point, and now that the change has started, there's no going back. Your body craves it like it craves air to breathe. If you don't feed it, it'll die."

My breathing picked up as my heart raced. "Maybe it's better that way..." My eyes locked on the small drip of blood flowing down his wrist. I could smell it and it was heavenly. I couldn't accurately describe the scent of his blood, but if I had to try, I'd compare it to rich dark chocolate.

"Better to die?" he asked, cocking his head to the side. His wound was already beginning to close up, and my window was fading.

"Why not?" I mumbled. "I almost did it once, would it be so hard?"

He stared at me for a few heartbeats, but all I could look at was the thin line of dripping blood. He took a deep breath and said, "You don't want to die, Serenity. You can spout that shit all you want, but I don't believe it for a second."

I huffed a bitter laugh. "What makes you such an expert all the sudden, huh? You don't know anything about me."

"I know enough," he said. "I know you were dealt a shitty hand."

I snorted outright. "Are you kidding me?"

"We've all had troubled pasts, Miss Harker. Believe it or not, the life of a vampire is a long one, and we all have our own histories and regrets. You're still young. You don't know what suffering is yet."

"Fuck you!" I barked as my belly simmered with anger. Who the fuck was he to tell me I hadn't suffered?

"Drink," he urged yet again, ignoring my outburst. "You'll die if you don't, and I really don't want to have to force it on you. But I will, make no mistake. I'll pry your pretty lips open and funnel my blood down your throat if you don't comply. I don't care if you don't want it. What you feel and what you want aren't important right now. So do yourself a favor and take it willingly." His voice was no longer soft or kind in any way.

I looked at myself in the reflection of that mask and saw the bags under my eyes and the red of my irises. I looked like the monsters humans warned their children about. I looked like a creature that ripped open throats. "I said fuck you." I kept my voice soft this time. Calm. Resigned.

Silence met my words as his vein closed up. The smell of his blood still filled the small room, but it wasn't anywhere near as potent as the remaining drips started to cool. Still, my throat was thick with it, and my teeth ached.

Lightning fast, he pressed me into the wall with his hand around my throat, squeezing until I could barely get any air. "Fuck me?" he seethed, hissing through his teeth. "Fuck me?! You want it that badly, I can fuck you right here against this wall." His fingers dug into my skin. "Is that what you really want, little dhampir? Because I'll give it to you. I'll fuck you so hard you forget your own name. Then maybe I'll drain you dry just for fun."

My heart and my mind was racing a mile a minute as I gasped for air. I tried to speak, tried to plead with the man, but I couldn't get a word out. My throat was closed, and I didn't know how much time I had left before I passed out.

With his free arm, he reached down under his mask, lifting it a hair, but not enough for me to see beneath it. I watched as he brought his wrist underneath, biting down hard and tearing into his own skin, sending rivulets of thick blood cascading down his arm. I squirmed, but there was nothing I could do. He was too strong. My only saving grace at the moment was the fact that I couldn't breathe and smell that delicious blood.

I didn't think he had it in him to be such a bastard, but I was dead wrong. The man shoved his bloodied wrist to my lips and pushed. Liquid filled my mouth—hot, thick and delicious. My eyes rolled, and I instantly came. My pussy clenched and my clit throbbed as the most intense orgasm of my life rolled over me. Wave after wave of ecstasy filled me up as I gulped in mouthfuls of the man's chocolate flavored blood.

I was moaning around his blood, slurping it down like I

couldn't get enough. His thigh was between the apex of my legs to keep me still, and I started to grind against it, needing that friction. Even though I'd just come, it hit me again in another wave. I was basically humping his leg now, and when I shifted my torso, I could feel the bulge of his hard cock against my stomach. As I ground myself against him, still sucking at his wrist, I heard him groan a guttural sound and watched with heated eyes as his head fell back slightly. I imagined his eyes were closed in pleasure.

All too soon, he was ripping his wrist from my mouth and staggering away. I hissed the second that blood flow was gone, and the sound was feral. Yanking against the chains, I heard the metal hook groan. The man continued to back up, his steps heavy and slightly staggered. I wondered if there was a limit to how much blood I could safely take from a vampire.

A surge of energy flowed through me as the blood settled inside of me, and it was like waking from a foggy dream. The crimson of his dripping wrist against the paleness of his skin was sparkling and stark, even in the low lightning. I could see dustmotes in the air, and I could clearly see into the other side of that dark window. The sound of the lights buzzing overhead was grating, and the smell of thick chocolaty blood permeated the air, making me want to leap from the wall and rip into the man again.

Atlas. I knew it was him. I could smell him—smoke and leather. It was the same man who had his face in my pussy at Rue, there was no question about it. He could hide all he wanted behind that mask, but he'd made a big mistake feeding me his blood. I could feel myself growing impossibly strong, and it was a fight to remain where I was. My limbs felt powerful enough that if I really tried, I might just be able to rip these chains from the wall. But I couldn't let him know that just yet.

There were things these men obviously knew about Ryan Harker, things I now wanted to know very much. Atlas had said Ryan had something of his that he wanted back, and I was determined to find out what that was. The time for games was over. My head was clearing, and the situation was becoming crisp and clear. It was time to stop fucking around.

He turned around, and I knew that any second, the lights would flicker off so he could leave out of whatever secret entrance they had built into the room, so I called out before he could disappear.

"Oh and, Atlas?" He staggered to a dead stop, shoulders stiffening. I watched as he slowly turned around to face me, no longer dripping blood. I smiled, but it was a mean, vengeful smile. It was a smile that promised the wrath of hell I was about to bring down on his head. "Leave the mask at the door next time. I'd like to see those bedroom eyes when you're forcing yourself on me."

He cursed, and then the lights went out.

CHAPTER 11
ATLAS

*S*lamming out of the holding cell, I left the guards to lock it back up again. They didn't question me as I fled, and it was a good thing because I was ready to rip some throats.

I staggered through the halls of the underground passageways far beneath the manor. It was dark down here, but I could see as clearly as if it were daylight. My cock was throbbing and my fangs were pulsing as I raced out of the labyrinth. Passing some of my coven members, I didn't bother to slow down, and several of them leapt out of the way in time for me to whir by.

I was in fucking pain. Agonizing pain. Every single molecule of my body was pulling me back to that padded cell. Back to the dhampir that had flipped the world on its head. I hadn't meant for it to go that far tonight. She still hadn't answered any of our questions. But it was impossible at times to keep my head straight when those depthless chocolate eyes were so probing and knowing.

I made it up three flights of stairs and staggered onto the

landing of our coven house. Luckily, the halls were mostly empty now that the sun had set. It was basically early morning for the vampires of Noc City. I raced up three more flights, reaching the top level of the mansion, reserved for the heads of the coven. My chambers were at the far end of the maze of hallways, far removed from any prying eyes or ears.

Slamming into the room, I locked the door behind me and immediately unzipped my pants. My cock was in my palm in seconds, and it was almost painful as I stroked it hard and fast. I'd never felt like this before. In my eight hundred years on this earth, I'd never felt such bone deep aching and longing. I was already coming in my palm, but it wasn't enough. In my mind's eye, I pictured her snowy white hair, saturated with thick blood that smelled like sugar. I pictured those slender fangs poking into her plump red lips and pumped faster. Groaning, I let thick ropes of cum coat my palms.

I remembered the first time I'd seen her in person at Rue, one of my many clubs throughout Noc City. I'd scented her the moment she arrived, and I'd known she was coming. I'd been waiting for her all evening. I hadn't planned on burying my face in her wet pussy, but sometimes, things couldn't be helped. The second I touched her supple skin, I knew I wanted to fuck her into oblivion in my small office that night, but alas, it wasn't to be quite yet. In a way, I guessed I was thankful for that.

I was so worked up, I failed to hear the clicking of my bedroom locks until it was too late and the door was swinging open. I didn't scramble to stop or shy away as Faust stepped into the room. He shut the door behind him and stared at me with eyes so dark, I swore I could see stars in them. My cock thickened.

It'd been this way between us off and on for a few years now. It'd started off as a friendship and eventually grew into something more. We still fucked women, many women, sometimes together and sometimes separate. Faust stalked closer with clear intent in his brown eyes before he grabbed me around the throat and hauled me against the wall. If any other vampire had done the same, I'd have ripped their head clean from their body in the blink of an eye.

His lips clashed with mine as we both groaned. His pierced tongue swiped against my own, and I bit down on his wide bottom lip, feeling especially volatile today. I was sure Faust could feel the tension in me ready to snap, because in the next breath, he dropped to his knees and took my cock in his mouth. I moaned and let my head fall against the bedroom door, closing my eyes as his piercing rolled over my sensitive head.

The exquisite thing about having another man suck your dick was that they knew all the perfect ways to do it. Hollowing his cheeks, I felt him suck harder, even going so far as to graze his incisors across my flesh. I started coming again, this time even harder. My dick slipped from his lips as I hauled him up and tossed him on my massive king sized bed. It wasn't hard to lift him. We were both big, burly bastards, but being as old as we were, we could lift a bus and still not break a sweat.

I stalked towards him, ripping off my shirt and letting the residual blood from my wrist drag over my torso. I watched Faust's eyes snag on the smear and darken. He unbuttoned his pants in record time and pulled his thick, pierced cock free. My mouth watered, and his wide lips tipped into a feral grin as he began to stroke himself.

"You visited her cell today," he said through clenched teeth.

I nodded, once more stroking myself as I approached. "I did. And I fed her my blood."

His eyes darkened, and I watched a muscle twitch in his jaw. I couldn't tell if it was anger or jealousy. Not about touching her, we didn't do the jealousy thing in that way, but that he hadn't been there to witness it. I knew he didn't particularly like the dhampir girl. His disdain for her was clear in the very mention of her name, but I also knew how his body responded to her. I'd seen him take off like a bat out of hell after leaving the padded room many times. I knew she affected him just as strongly as me.

"And?" he asked.

"And she's strong," I said with a frown. "Very strong."

His eyes lit up for a moment. It had been a gamble, playing with her life this way. Dhampirs were volatile creatures, and it could have gone one of two ways. Either she grew strong and her immortality kicked in, or it was too late and the bloodlust would send her into a feral frenzy that would eventually kill her. I shouldn't have gambled with her life like that, but it was too late for me to care. There were lives on the line here, and not just hers.

I made it to the bed and knelt, grasping his cock in my palm. His head tilted back and dropped to the mattress, along with his wide shoulders. I heard him groan lazily as I gripped him tight, running the pad of my thumb under the swollen tip. Before he could say anything else, I closed my lips over the head of his thick cock and sucked, drawing a guttural moan from his lips. Every time I heard those noises, shivers racked my body.

Faust was the first man I'd ever been sexual with. I'd never considered myself bisexual, not in the entire eight centuries I'd been around. I'd never given it a single thought until I met Faust back in the early nineteen-twenties. He'd come to the States from Europe sometime in the early eighteenth century and joined the Nocturne Coven in the twenties. He was old, nearly as old as myself, and we'd instantly bonded. He became my right-hand man soon after, and it was like the connection formed all on its own. Eventually, I found myself thinking about him in ways I'd never entertained before in regards to another man.

We'd fucked for the first time just ten years ago, on a night at one of our seedier clubs downtown. We'd been drunk on the blood of a few human women who'd come to party, but ended up fucking in my office by the end of the night. That night changed me in ways I still had yet to come to terms with. We weren't a couple, not in the traditional sense, but we were closer than coven members. He was still my right-hand man, and I liked to think I was his.

I sucked harder and pumped his shaft as he started to come in my mouth. I swallowed him down as he cursed, placing his palms over his eyes as his legs shook beneath me. I removed my mouth from his cock and sank my fangs into the flesh of his inner thigh and sucked, drawing out yet another guttural curse from Faust.

His hot blood poured down the sides of my mouth as my eyes rolled back in my head. He tasted like spearmint and honey. I couldn't take much, as vampires normally didn't drink each other's blood. It was like a drug, of sorts. It gave us a high, but served no actual purpose. Not like a dhampir's blood. As I drank, I pictured Serenity in my mind's eye, pictured her lips closing over my wrist as she drank for the first time.

I pictured her eyes glossing over in feral need as her nipples pebbled against her night dress. I wanted to fuck that woman in every way imaginable. I craved the feel of that tight pussy around my cock and wondered how it would feel to take her tight ass while Faust fucked her pussy at the same time. We'd done it with other women in the past, but the thought of Serenity between us had me salivating.

We hadn't known she was a dhampir when we took her from the edge of that bridge. At the time, she'd only been the bitchy daughter of the senator responsible for stealing my sister away from the coven. She was culpable in all of his crimes, guilty by association. But the moment Merrick had tasted her blood and staggered away, we knew exactly what she was and what this meant. Dhampirs were incredibly rare, but they were special in many ways. They could walk in the sun and eat human food. They could choose immortality or refrain forever, choosing to live a human lifespan.

I'd taken that choice from her tonight. I knew I should feel guilty about it, but I honestly didn't. Regardless of the fact that she was half-vampire, there was no telling just how much she knew about the business her father was neck deep into. For all we knew, she could be lying to us. There was a very real possibility that she knew the location of each holding facility and knew exactly what they were doing with the missing women. Loxley was the only other dhampir in our coven, aside from a five-year-old girl named Celeste. Loxely was my half-sister and a product of my sire and some human woman he'd bedded for a short time centuries ago. I'd let her slip through my fingers.

I licked my tongue across the wound on Faust's inner thigh and watched it close up before standing. I buttoned my pants and joined him on my massive bed, letting myself fall backwards, then stared at the ceiling. He was buttoning his own pants as he said, "There was an incident today."

I glance at him, heart sinking in my chest. "What happened?"

He and Merrick were still posing as the senator's new bodyguards. They'd been in some pretty deep shit for letting Serenity be taken away, but he'd kept them on staff all the same. It was risky, but it was worth it for the information they might gather. Luckily, we had connections to Bastian, a local warlock selling daylight potion on the black market. It was some nasty shit and only held for around ten hours at a time, but it served its purpose and passed my men off as humans.

"The video we leaked in the city center caused a riot," said Faust, his voice grave and thick. I watched him as he frowned up at the ceiling. "They killed two wolf pups right there in front of me, and there was nothing I could do to stop it."

"Fuck," I breathed, running a hand down my tired face. "Which pack?"

"The Blood Moon Pack, I think," he murmured. "They were young, teenagers. I don't even think they were old enough to shift yet."

"Shit," I added, stomach sinking. This was a problem. Those pups shouldn't have been anywhere near Harker's supporters. They were wolves, yes, but before their first shift, they were still vulnerable, and humans together in an angry mob could do some damage to even the most mature wolves. "I'll have a talk with their alpha." I shuddered, not looking forward to speaking with him. They were wild and unhinged sometimes, especially when it came to the murder of one of their own.

"Won't do any good," Faust said darkly. "When August finds out, he's going to unleash hell on this city."

He was right. August, Blood Moon's alpha was a wild card. At over a thousand years old, he was still mateless and had a thirst for blood and war the likes of which I hadn't seen since the warlords of ancient times. Losing a few pups at the hands of human radicals was just the spark that would light the fire that could burn the city to the ground. I knew it was only a matter of time until August came calling on my coven to assist.

"I'm sorry, man," I said numbly.

He shook his head and waved me off in that typical Faust fashion of his. Always stoic. Always dead inside. "It is what it is." But it wasn't, and we both knew that.

We sat there in silence for the next half hour, soaking up the quiet darkness while we still could. I knew things were about to change, but deep down, I knew it was more than time for it. The humans were gaining too much power, and they needed to be snuffed out before they could ignite Noc City. This was about to get ugly.

CHAPTER 12
SERENITY

I woke to the image of Ryan Harker staring at me from that pane of glass. His watery blue eyes held no pity and no mercy in them. The moment I cracked my eyes open, I knew these chains would no longer hold me. Strength and power coursed through my veins now, but I stayed put.

"Your plan backfired," he said, breaking the silence with a smug smirk. He wasn't looking at me. I glanced to my left and found two of the masked men standing there with their arms crossed over their chests. To my right was another, only...he wasn't wearing a mask.

"And how do you figure that?" Atlas Nocturne asked, hands in the pockets of his crisp black suit that fit him to perfection. Tattoos snaked up and over his neck, at odds with the regal attire and gleaming dress shoes. That same diamond watch I'd seen at Rue glinted in the red light.

A sliver of satisfaction rolled through me at seeing his face. I'd caught him on my own. He thought that mask and that voice box would be enough to fool me, but I wasn't an idiot, and he wasn't as careful as he thought.

I watched as Ryan took a sip from a glass of something amber colored and smiled after a thin swallow. "They riot in the streets on behalf of my beloved daughter." His eyes flickered to mine, and I fought a gag, remembering his hands on my skin. "I feel like I should send you a token of my appreciation. You did half the work for me."

I frowned... What was he talking about? Riots in the streets? My eyes went back to that blinking red light.

Still, despite the taunting, Atlas was smiling at Ryan when I looked back over at him. I arched a brow, wondering what the hell his angle was. Ryan was right—they'd played right into his hands. My former father was a cunning man, always thinking twelve steps ahead. If the public knew I was missing, or if these recordings had been released, there would be riots. Much to my annoyance, the humans of Noc City adored me. Actually, all over the state, they worshiped my father and thought I was his perfect, angelic daughter, the poster girl for what all women should aspire to be.

Atlas walked towards the image of Ryan Harker. "But how would your adoring fans react if they were to find out your dirty little secret?"

Silence met his question. I watched Ryan's face, and it didn't move an inch. He didn't even twitch. But there...in the depths of those eyes was a flicker of unease. Atlas had hit the nail right on the head. Though I was still at the mercy of these men, I couldn't help but revel in the feeling of smugness that brought me.

He smiled as he added, "See, I'm not too sure your loyal followers would be so keen on you harboring a dhampir all this time, parading her around like some kind of trophy. Why, I'd hazard a guess they'd be downright..." He feigned searching for the right word before he finished with, "Enraged." Then he grinned.

One of the other men took a step forward, and I watched the grace with which he moved to stand next to Atlas. "It's your move, Senator. Tell us what we need to know, and we'll send the girl home." My gut twinged at the thought of being released to that monster again. "Where are the facilities?"

Silence once more as Ryan stared straight at me, ignoring the men entirely. His lips stretched into a forced smile, and I instantly felt like vomiting. After too many heartbeats, he looked back at Atlas. "Your threats mean nothing to me, bloodsucker. You tell the world my wife's a whore who spawned an abomination, and it'll only fuel their hatred for your kind. I'll throw Elodie to the wolves and claim I knew nothing of it."

Goddamn, he was a bastard. A fucking psychotic bastard. I may not like my mom even on good days, but I didn't want to see her thrown out on the streets and disgraced. She'd be ripped apart. For the most part, I'd been kept away from the violence on the streets and sheltered from the realities of this race war running rampant for years on end. But I knew my mother wouldn't last a day out there on her own.

Atlas was still grinning. Even wider now, actually. This caused Ryan's smug expression to falter, though I could tell by the tight line around his mouth that he was struggling to hide it.

"Unfortunately for you, Senator, we thought ahead." Atlas raised a ring clad hand, pinching a small rectangle between his fingers and waving it slightly. "We've taken the liberty of recording this entire conversation, just in case you decided to pull some of your usual bullshit." Ryan's face went ashen, and Atlas added, "So think very hard about your next move, because all it'll take is the press of a button, and this conversation will be blasted all over the country."

Ryan went to open his mouth again, but the still masked man cut him off first. "You have twenty-four hours to decide. Come clean about the facilities, or watch your empire crumble." They didn't give Ryan a chance to respond before Atlas pointed the remote at the screen and shut it off.

The room descended into silence once more, and the men just stood there. The tallest man on my left stood stock still, opening and closing his fists, and the only sound in the room was that of his leather gloves rubbing together.

"So who's going to tell—"

A hand was around my throat once again in the blink of an eye as one of the masked men held me against the wall. My eyes were wide in the mirrored surface as he seethed, "You're going to tell me everything you know about the facilities. Where they are, who's running them, and how we get there!"

I pretended to cough around the hold he had on my throat. Yesterday, this hold might have stifled my air, but after drinking Atlas' blood, I was feeling strong. My muscles tightened, preventing him from blocking my airway, but he was too riled up to notice. Still, I pretended to struggle. I needed information, and if they thought I was weak, then I'd have a better chance of finding out what the fuck was going on.

I coughed as I squeaked out, "I don't know...what you're talking—"

"Don't you lie to me, bitch!"

"I'm—" I coughed again and thrashed my head for extra oomph. "I don't know what facility you're talking about." He lightened up his hold, and I took that as my cue to speak again. "I swear, I don't know what you mean. What facilities?"

"You think I'm falling for the innocent princess act?" he spat. "You've been right there by the senator's side since the day you were born. You and your filthy humans are all the same, and you need to stop playing with us."

"I'm not a human," I retorted petulantly. "I thought we established that."

"Human enough," he snarled, bringing his face even closer. My nose was brushing the surface of the mask now. "Two wolves died on my watch this morning." My heart lurched to my throat, not understanding. "Two young men were gunned down in broad daylight because of your father and his followers. It'll keep happening if you don't tell us what we need to bring him down for good."

I didn't know what facilities he was talking about. My father—Ryan had never told me anything about his official business. I was there to look pretty and smile, not to have input or opinions.

"Let's go," Atlas said, breaking through the thick tension. The man looked over at the coven leader. "We have a meeting with the Blood Moon Pack in a few hours and can't be late."

"What...You can't just keep me in here forever," I snapped. "I don't know shit about a facility. I'm of no use to you."

"Bullshit—"

Atlas cut off the man with a hand on his arm. The masked man was tense, and I could see the way his hands shook. Those wolves getting killed really messed with him, and in some sick way, I sort of pitied him. I felt for him, even though I really shouldn't have, not as I hung here on the wall in chains.

Atlas had one of the other men take me off the wall and chain me to the same spot in the center of the room again. My arms tingled, but I wasn't aching like I would have had I not been high on blood for the first time in my life as a dhampir.

My body still felt invigorated, and I knew I was strong enough to break these chains. Still, I waited. I waited for hours and hours, bored out of my mind. I found myself thinking about Trix and how frantic she had to be right now. I wished there was a way I could reach her and tell her I was still alive and relatively unscathed, all things considered. Knowing her, she'd riled up enough supporters to launch a full scale investigation, since I had no doubt Ryan hadn't lifted a finger. I just hoped my cousin was smart enough not to point fingers and get herself into trouble.

The lights went off and then back on again, and a masked man was in front of me. I hated when they did that. Blinking, I just stared at him in silence, and he stared right back. This one wasn't Atlas. No, this one was significantly taller than the coven leader. His chest was broader, shoulders and biceps massive. I looked him up and down, curious.

"Why am I still here?" I asked, breaking the quiet of the padded room. He stared at me, not saying a word. It was unnerving being unable to read his facial expressions. I sighed, deep and weary. "I'm getting tired of this cloak and dagger bullshit. The masks were spooky the first few days, but now I'm just annoyed." If I could have crossed my arms over my chest, I would have.

He took a step forward and my belly flipped, but I watched unamused as he moved slowly, crouching into a squat position with his forearms over his bent knees. "You think you're the only one who tires of this?" My breath caught as that deep voice rumbled out. The voice box made it scratchy and rough, but there was something about the cadence...

"You realize I know nothing, right?" I asked. "By now, you have to realize you bet on the wrong horse."

His shoulders rose and fell steadily as he said, "Not entirely, Miss Harker." Once again, there was something off about his words. It was harder to understand this man than it was with the other two. "There's something you need to know."

My pulse sped up. Finally, we were getting somewhere. He was only half right, though. There were a whole hell of a lot of things I needed to know, but I'd settle for anything at this point. I stared at him, waiting for him to elaborate.

He sighed when I raised an impatient brow and said, "The disappearances... Are you familiar with them?"

I frowned, not expecting that in the slightest. But yes, I knew what he was asking about immediately. The famous disappearances. Women had been going missing all over the city, and there were no leads or traces. Ryan hadn't made any public statements regarding the women, due to the fact that they were all darklings, but it was a well-known fact, even amongst the humans. Something was happening to darkling women, and the police were looking the other way.

I nodded, so he continued, "What you might not know is that every single darkling female who's gone missing is a half-blood." I sucked in a breath. "Species doesn't seem to matter, but all of them were half-darkling, half-human."

I knew there were more like me all over the city. As much animosity as there was between the darklings and the humans, it wasn't exactly rare for them to couple up every now and then, and even more so after factions of humans began advocating on the darklings' behalf. Over the years, more and more humans had grown close to darkling communities and immersed themselves in activism efforts to uphold the Coexist Doctrine. Despite the factions of humans who called for segregation, they didn't speak for all of them.

"And you think Ryan has something to do with these disappearances?" I asked, putting it together easily. I knew immediately I was right. Did Ryan have something to do with these women going missing? What facilities was he talking about?

He cocked his head. "How long have you known he wasn't your biological father?"

The question momentarily threw me off, and for a second, I considered not answering, but thought *what the hell*. There was nothing left for me to lose anyway. "Twelve months," I said solemnly, eyes glossing over in memory. "You might have heard about the assassination attempt at city hall?" He nodded. It was a needless question, as my near death and my brother's murder were still front page news across the country.

My breath came out shakily as I remembered that horrible day. "When the bombs went off, it was supposed to be a distraction, something to pull our bodyguards away for a split second." I remembered the fear and the panic in those short moments. I remembered standing there one minute, listening to my father speak at the podium, bored out of my mind and squeezing Sean's hand three times, and the next moment... "They didn't mention it on the news, but a bullet hit me in the chest that day."

The man's shoulders tightened with this new information. I frowned at him, wondering why that bothered him in the slightest. Or maybe he was wondering how he hadn't had all the information. Nobody outside of our immediate circle knew about that. I'd been swept out of reach of the cameras and chaos so quickly that my blood was mistaken for Sean's.

"I was hit once, but it missed my heart, hitting a little too far right, but Sean—" My voice caught. I looked down towards my wrists as I itched at the tight cuffs. "A bullet went straight through his neck. Blood went everywhere—on my hands and clothes and my face. I didn't realize until later that some of it must have gone in my mouth."

In fact, it took me a week to realize this, as my wounds from that day had healed up in a matter of hours. The doctors had been sworn to secrecy, or maybe they'd just been killed to ensure their silence. The human blood entering my bloodstream…there was no way of hiding it.

"My mom wasn't there that day. She was organizing the charity event for the next night in Sol City. So when I was taken into surgery, the only one here to donate blood was my father." I could remember the frantic pace of every-thing that day. It was like a swift, blurry slideshow flick-ering before my eyes. Nothing was concrete, but I remembered the taste of fear and confusion, I remembered wondering where Sean was. My mother wouldn't make it back to Noc for hours, even by plane, as Sol City—a witch-run haven on the other side of the country—was too far away.

"You can probably guess what happened after that," I said to the man.

"His blood wasn't compatible," he guessed, and I nodded my head.

"That's how he found out I wasn't his. When I managed to make a full recovery in less than three days, he also realized how big of a lie his wife had been keeping from him. A bastard child…an abomination."

"And no one knows because the senator is too proud to admit his wife stepped out on him with a vampire," he concluded for himself.

The days following that little revelation had been hell on earth. When my mother came back to find her son dead from a bullet to the throat and her daughter miraculously recovered, she knew it was all over for her. I'd expected Ryan to throw us out on our asses and tell the whole world our secret. I'd expected a lot of things that never happened. Instead, the world mourned my brother as the story made national news.

"My mom was forced to go on camera and plead for the terrorists to come forward. My recovery was hailed a miracle, and I was threatened into smiling for photo ops, pretending like my life hadn't exploded around me. Pretending like the most important person in my life hadn't been brutally ripped away…" Sean's absence was like a hole in my heart that continued to ache.

Sean was gone forever, and the general consensus was that I'd been the primary target. Sean and I were the only ones shot that day, which didn't make any sense. Ryan was in clear view of the shooter, and I was slightly behind him. Someone tried to kill me specifically, but Sean got in the way. Ryan's PR team spun the story that it was the Nocturne Coven attempting to assassinate the Angel of Noc City, trying to start a war. The feud between the humans and the vampires ran deep and bloody, and this attempt was the declaration they needed. But I had my doubts.

I huffed a bitter sounding laugh, "He made sure she paid for it, though." My eyes darkened, and I swore I could feel phantom bruises resurfacing. I felt the man's gaze burning through me, as if even behind that mask, he could see past this flimsy dress to the silvery slashes marking my back.

My mind went back to those months after we buried Sean. The nights when the cameras were turned off, and it was just me, Mom, and Ryan in the mansion. The nights he'd beat her in front of me, and the housekeeping staff had to mop up the blood and keep quiet. I remembered the torture of smelling her blood as it splattered the pristine white walls. The way he'd taunt me and throw my helplessness in my face. All the while, my mom just sat there and let it all happen, knowing it was all her fault. I remembered vividly the nights he'd catch me alone and make sure I remembered it the next morning with bruises that had to be covered with makeup and expensive clothing.

It wasn't long until Carson was included in the small number of people who knew my secret. I was afraid at first that he'd turn away from me and tell the world, but it never happened. Carson continued fucking me night after night, telling me about his plans to make me his wife... His little dhampir whore. I let that man put his dick in me too many times, and my stomach churned just thinking about it.

"I'm sorry you had to witness that," he said, softer than I thought possible.

I blinked at him, catching myself from telling him that I didn't just witness it. In all honesty, my mom got off easy. I still hadn't told her the extent of the beatings I'd taken, not only from him, but from Carson and even some of the men they employed. My mother had been forced to punish me as well, but sometimes, I thought she preferred it, if only to lessen the pain she knew he'd make me feel had he done it himself. Then she'd go get drunk for a few days and pretend I didn't exist. I healed faster than a human, so there was never any evidence or proof, and my bodyguards just looked away.

"I don't need your sorry," I snapped. "I need you to tell me what you want from me now that you know the truth. If I knew something, believe me, I'd tell you, but I just don't." At this point, I was starting to wish I'd been closer to my father's work. If he was doing something shady, I had no clue.

"You must remember something from your time with the senator," he said. I looked up, staring at my reflection in his mask. "You had to have heard or seen something that wasn't right. A conversation, a weird visitor even." His voice was tight, and again, hard to understand. I was beginning to work out that he had a thick accent. "Miss Harker—"

"Serenity," I corrected, clenching my jaw tight. "Harker was never my name." In fact, I didn't know what my true last name was. I didn't think I'd ever know. I wondered if my father was a member of Nocturne...in which case, he would've adopted the last name Nocturne as all coven members do. Was I a Nocturne? Or perhaps my father was just a coward or a nomad. Either way, he was just as much of a bastard as Ryan.

After a long pause, he said, "Serenity." My chest tightened, detecting a bit of softness that wasn't there before. "I'm asking you for anything." I squinted up at him as he added, "Atlas has a half-sister. Her name is Loxely. She's about your age and a dhampir too. She's one of the women who went missing a few months back." *Shit.* This was personal. "We have every reason to believe she's still alive, but we need to know where she and the others are being held."

"And I've told you I have no idea. I wouldn't even know where to start. Ryan never told me anything. Maybe if I'd been a son, he'd have told me something, but he was secretive about business. Even if Sean had known about any kind of darkling prison, I know he would have told me. We didn't keep secrets from each other."

"I'm beginning to believe that, Serenity, but there has to be something you can give us to point us in the right direction," he said gravely. "There's no telling what's being done to them. The senator has friends in some pretty low places, and there have been rumors…"

"What kind of rumors?" I asked, stomach filling with dread.

He breathed a heavy sigh, and it struck me that this was perhaps the most human-like behavior I'd observed in any of these men thus far. Although, that probably wasn't a fair observation, as I couldn't rightly hold them to that standard. "Inside sources have suggested patents on an untested drug have been filed outside of the Coexist Doctrine's jurisdiction. There's been chatter about a man named Dr. Fabian Bellamy. Have you heard of him?"

Bile rose in my throat. My heart leapt in my chest, and despite the chill of the room, I could feel small beads of sweat sprouting up on the back of my neck. Bellamy…I knew him. I knew Fabian Bellamy well. He'd been there to pry the bullet from my chest that day. He'd been there to declare what I was, one of the only people on the planet who knew what I was. I'd been poked and prodded by that monster more times than I could count over the last year, just a curiosity to him, a freak. I never liked the old man, even before the attack. I always thought he was a creep.

The man in front of me stiffened, obviously taking my wide eyed, pale silence as answer to his question. "Thought so," he said and blew out a long breath.

"What about him?" I asked, voice gravelly. I was nauseous all of a sudden.

"We have reason to believe Dr. Bellamy is heading the study and preliminary trials of the unsanctioned drug, and we think it has a connection to the disappearances."

"How?" It didn't make any sense. These were only speculations, random scattered pieces to a puzzle that might not even exist. "How can you know that for sure?"

He sighed, shoulders dropping as he said, "Because one of the women was found in the woods just outside of pack territory. A wolf girl, no older than sixteen, who'd gone missing early last year. Her autopsy showed traces of a foreign drug in her bloodstream that caused her body to behave…irregularly." That last part was said with a slight hiss, and I arched a brow.

"What does that mean?"

"She was…" He shook his head, as if struggling for the words. "She was human."

It felt like the world dropped out from beneath me. Human. But how? It didn't make sense. Unlike some vampires, wolves weren't made the same way. A vampire could be born or they could be turned, but werewolves and witches were only born. Yes, there were half-bloods born to both humans and wolves, but they were still natural wolves. A bite wouldn't turn you the way human tall tales once thought. The shifting gene was carried down through family bloodlines, which was the main reason wolf packs were so tightly knit and reclusive. Half-blood wolves were rare, but the genes were embedded in their very DNA.

"Before she died, she whispered one single name, and it was that tip that gave us the lead we needed to hunt these facilities down."

"Bellamy," I muttered.

He nodded. "Her blood was tested, and no matter how many times they repeated it, not a single shifting enzyme was found. Just gone, as if she were nothing more than a regular human."

"So you think it was the drug that changed her?" I asked. "Why would someone want to change a wolf?"

He barked a laugh that caught me off guard as he straightened. "Yeah, I guess someone like you wouldn't have a clue, would you?' He laughed again. "You've been pampered and sheltered all your life, lass, but out in the real world, darklings are basically animals. Why would anyone want to turn a wolf into a human? I'll give ya one fucking guess."

"I wasn't—" *Holy shit. Holy shit, holy shit! Lass?* He'd fucked up. He'd fucked up big time letting that slip, because I suddenly knew the man behind the mask, and I could take a wild fucking guess who the other one was.

"I don't give a shit," he said, not realizing that I was screaming inside my head. He stood back up to his full height, and I wanted to bang my head against the wall for not recognizing him before. "I'll give you a while to think about this new information. Atlas will be back soon, so I'd think real hard on it if I were you."

Anger surged through me. Anger and betrayal. How dare they tie me up like an animal after they watched what I'd gone through at the Badgley estate? He'd been standing right there, watching those men fondle me, and did nothing to protect me. Without another word, he turned, and I knew any second, the lights would go out and he'd be gone again, so I moved faster than I'd ever moved before.

The decision was made before I even realized it. The cuffs and chains binding me to the floor fell away like pieces of clay. The room was a blur as I launched myself at him, and I heard a whoosh of breath leave his lungs when our bodies connected and we tumbled to the cushioned ground. I was frantic, punching, kicking, and clawing at him while I shouted profanities left and right. My words were a mixture of hissing and screaming. He blocked my blows, twisting this way and that, and I could already tell that once the surprise wore off, I'd be done for. I might be a half-breed vampire, but I had a feeling he was much older and much stronger.

As he was spinning us around, hands like steel vices, I curled my fingers under the edge of his mirrored mask, watching one last time as fury filled my red eyes, and ripped it off his face, tearing the black hood with it. The mask went flying across the room, and the man yelled, "Fuck!" as he fumbled for my wrists. I struggled, but I was growing tired. I was pretty sure I'd expended most of my newly acquired energy busting out of those chains, and now I was coming down from the rush.

"Why don't you call for your friends, you fucking prick?!" I shouted in his face. "Where's Faust, huh?! Where the hell is he? Motherfucker, I can't believe this shit. You were supposed to protect me!"

He stilled, hands wrapped securely around my wrists, pinning them to the cushioned ground. He stared at me, face close enough for me to pick out each and every freckle dotting his familiar face. The hairs of his beard brushed my lips, and I hated myself for the little flip in my stomach. Where I expected grass green eyes, I only saw deep crimson surrounded by inky black rather than whites—vampire eyes. Eyes like mine. Eyes like Atlas.

"Hello, Merrick, you bastard," I spat, giving my wrists a useless tug. "I should have known..."

"But you didn't, did you?" Merrick hissed, lips twitching

upwards into a bitter smile. "You're exceptionally unobservant for a dhampir, did you know that?" His breath washed over my face, smelling of tobacco and mint. "I can smell your sweetness from a mile away..." Dipping his face, I stilled as he ran his nose up the side of my exposed neck. "Your senses are dull and your wits seem to have escaped you, lass. Pity it took ya this long to work it out."

"Get off me," I gritted through my teeth. I wasn't really struggling anymore, all the fight drained from my body now, but he didn't let up. Merrick inhaled at my neck, and I felt a shudder roll through his massive body that covered mine from head to toe.

"Honey," he whispered, words fanning over my skin. "You smell like the sweetest honey. Makes me wonder if you taste as sweet."

"You fucking bastard," I growled. "Get off me." I was no longer yelling. I didn't have the energy for it.

"You need more blood," he said, lifting his head to meet my stare. His eyes dipped to my lips for a brief moment before rising again. "You can take it from me, little dhampir," he offered. "I don't mind. Wouldn't want me to have the upper hand all the time, now would we?"

"I'd rather die," I deadpanned, not breaking eye contact.

"What's this obsession with dying you seem to have these days?" He chuckled darkly. "I was beginning to think the bridge was a one off, but now, I'm not so sure." His smile was bitter and cold as he added, "If you don't drink again soon, I promise you'll get that wish."

Unease ran through me because I knew he wasn't lying. The bloodlust was in me now, and there was no going back. I'd die without more blood.

"It won't be a pretty death," he said. His lips were hovering over mine now as I clamped my mouth shut tight.

My fingers flexed, veins losing circulation under his grip. "It could take months, you know. Has anyone ever explained the process?" I blinked, choosing not to respond, knowing he'd tell me anyway. Strands of his long auburn hair fell from the loose bun and brushed his shoulders before hanging down to sweep my cheeks. "Your body will start to shut down and eat itself. Your veins will dry up, and your mind will desiccate. I hear it's quite painful."

Raw fear slithered up my spine at the mental image. I knew he was trying to scare me, but it was working. I could tell he was telling the truth, and I could tell he knew that I knew, because he smiled wider. Merrick's fingers were still wrapped around my wrists, and with my palms facing upwards, it left room for his thumbs to brush circles against my upturned palms. The silky touch of them made me dizzy.

Despite his threats and the wicked gleam in those blood-thirsty eyes, I could feel the unmistakable press of a hard bulge against me. Our hips were aligned, and apparently, whatever was happening here was turning him on. His cock was growing harder by the second, and I had a feeling he knew I was aware of that but didn't care at all.

"Cut the shit, Merrick," I said. "How did you hide it?"

"Hide what?"

"You know what," I spat.

"Oh you mean this?" His lips spread into a smile as two long, sharp fangs gleamed back at me. My belly flipped again. "A bit of magic goes a long way," he said. "You humans are so easy to manipulate." I frowned. Magic did this? I'd never heard of such a thing. And that would imply the vampires were working closely with a witch or a warlock... What kind of arrangement would that entail?

"I'm not a—"

"Oh, but aren't you?" he asked. "You've been a dhampir for a year, but it doesn't make you one of us, princess." His smile was gone now. "You spent your whole life behind the man who waged war on my kind. You were content to live comfortably behind those expensive walls. You think just because your whore moth—"

I lunged, craning my neck forward as a hiss escaped my lips. My teeth stretched and elongated as a cold fury filled me. Merrick pulled back with a grin. "Don't like that, lass? Is the truth too much for your delicate sensibilities?"

"Fuck you, Merrick!" I wanted nothing more to punch him in the teeth and see those fangs snap right off. I might not like my mother, but the only one allowed to call her what she was, was me. He didn't know her story. He didn't know what she and I had gone through. Hell, I barely knew the truth for myself, but I wasn't about to let some prick call her a whore.

"Not in a million years," he deadpanned. "You think I'm a weak man?" He thrust his hips forward, and I held back a squeak of shock, trying to ignore the thrill of pleasure that shot through me at the contact. I refrained from rolling my hips. "You think because you have a tight pussy and a fuck-able mouth that I'll buckle? Sweetheart, you overestimate yourself."

"Then why don't you get off me?" I suggested. "Either kill me or let me go, but I'm sick of this shit already. I've seen your face now, so you know there's only two ways this can end."

Merrick went utterly still above me, just staring unnervingly into my eyes. I searched his gaze, trying to locate any ounce of morality inside him, but I couldn't see it. A predator looked back at me. A predator full of rage and loathing and centuries worth of distrust. I'd never known a vampire before, not personally. Trix and I had been to Rue a few times, so I brushed shoulders with them, but it wasn't until now that I realized how dangerous they really were. Even with the monster inside me waking up and thrashing around, it was jarring to see such power staring back at me.

"Come on, Merrick," I taunted, lips stretching into a tight smile that I didn't feel deep down. "Or do you have to wait for orders? Are you Atlas' whipping boy?'

"Watch yourself, little dhampir, You go too far," he purred, voice laced with danger. I was pushing him, but I didn't care anymore.

I tilted my head to the side and said, "Your eyes tell me you want to rip out my throat and watch my blood spill all over this room." His red eyes grew darker, and I felt his grip flex on my wrists. I smiled wider. "But your cock against my pussy feels like you need something else..."

A hiss fell from his lips, feral, dark and dangerous. His dick hardened even more if it were possible, and his hips rolled against mine. It was all I could do to contain a moan. I'd always been a sexual person and never tried to shy away from the things my body craved. For years, Carson had been the only outlet for that need, and even though I loathed the man to my very core, he'd scratched that itch. But Merrick... he was another story altogether. He was a man I shouldn't want. It was despicable to even consider fucking one of my captors.

But the thrill of the thought was almost too much to ignore. As a vampire, my senses were heightened. Every human need or want was amplified, even though I was a half-blood. Vampires and wolves were known for their sex drives. It was just one of the many reasons the humans called them animals. I guessed I was an animal then, because I could feel the vampire side of me reaching out for

Merrick with extended claws. I wanted to tear him apart and make myself feel something.

Merrick's eyes took on a strange gleam the longer we stared at each other. He was messing with me...but then again, was he? I could both see and feel the way his body wanted me. It would be so easy too. In the slip dress, all he'd have to do is pull himself free and drive himself home. It was startling when I realized that had he done just that, I would've let him. I could almost feel it—the slide of his thick cock against my center. The fullness of him driving deep inside me over and over again. I'd scratch my claws down his back, tearing the skin. I'd bite down into the flesh of his shoulder...

"What a naughty little Angel of Noc City," Merrick purred, face descending closer to mine. His fingers on my wrist were tight and unrelenting, and his hips pinned me in place. "Let's get something straight right now, Serenity." I hissed as he whispered my name huskily. "I'm no one's errand boy. If I want to fuck you into oblivion right here, right now, then I will. Not a soul could stop me."

My eyes were glued to his lips as he spoke. They were incredibly inviting the way they formed each accented word. The deep brogue rolled off his tongue like silken honey, and the flash of fang when he grinned nearly had me coming right there. I hated this feeling, this wanting deep inside me, but I knew all I had to do was let the monster inside me take over.

Before I could reply with something snarky, his lips captured mine. It wasn't a soft brush, or a teasing lick. It was violent. I kissed him back as he pumped his hips into mine, grinding against me. The friction between us had me squirming, ready to combust. His mouth probed mine and he tasted the way he smelled, like rich tobacco and mint.

The scratch of his beard tickled my cheeks, and I loved it. Moaning into his mouth caused him to do the same, and I took a sliver of satisfaction that I had the power to make this creature come undone, even for a few short minutes.

Primal need was filling me up, setting my very skin on fire. He released my wrists, and I supposed I could've taken that chance to flee. I could've ripped away and knocked him out, but I still wasn't completely sure how much strength it would take to incapacitate a full-blooded vampire. Instead, I took what I needed. I allowed myself to indulge in all the things my body craved. I kissed him harder, to the point that I tasted blood in my mouth. His blood. It was sweeter than chocolate and made my veins buzz with energy. I needed more.

Ripping my face away, he reared his head back to look directly in my eyes, breathing hard and fast, eyes red and glazed over in lust. His fangs bit into his lip, and a dribble of blood, either mine or his, leaked out from the side of his mouth. The sight made me crave more. "You don't know what you're asking, little dhampir," he husked in that deep brogue.

"Don't tell me what I want, *vampire*."

"You want to be fucked?" he asked, smirking darkly. "In your prison cell? Because I can do that right here and now, and I won't regret a thing." His palm ran down my inner arm, elongated fingernail slicing a thin line down my pearly skin. I watched as little beads of crimson began to drip away from the incision. It didn't hurt in the slightest.

"You would fuck your prisoner?" I asked, cocking my head to the side. "What would Atlas have to say about that?" I was taunting him, and I could feel his muscles bunching, hardening.

"Atlas does not speak for me, lass. You need to know that

before we go any further. Your humans might bow down to their leaders, but vampires take what they want."

"And what is it that you want, Merrick?" I practically purred his name and watched in sick satisfaction as his eyes grew a shade darker.

At the sound of his name, the look of what I could only describe as ancient and feral hunger crossed his face. For a moment, I felt like I caught a glimpse of who he really was. I knew he was old. Older than this city, older than this country perhaps. I knew he'd seen things I couldn't even imagine. He'd probably fought wars I'd only ever read about and fucked countless women in his lifetime. But I only saw it all for a split second before that hunger made my former bodyguard lose control.

In a blur of movement, I was yanked up from the floor and hauled against the padded wall. The air whooshed out of my chest, but I didn't have time to say a word or utter a sound before his lips had mine again. My hands snaked into his now unbound bronze hair that fell in tangled waves to his shoulders. Then I clawed farther down, ripping at his hoodie, hearing the fabric shred under the force of my new strength. He was shirtless in seconds, and I wished I had the time to properly appreciate him, to take in every detail of his sculpted body. I could feel it under the pads of my fingers and wanted to run my tongue along every inch.

When my nails elongated and I could feel my teeth throbbing, I scratched down the front of his chest to his rigid abdomen, eliciting a deep growl. He moved faster than I could track, slamming my wrists against the wall. I heard a clicking sound and soon, both arms were overhead and chained to the wall once more. I flexed my wrist and knew that if I really wanted to, I could break free of the cuffs. They could no longer hold me here, and I think he knew that. But

I smiled as he stood back, staring at me with eyes as dark as my soul.

Merrick stalked forward slowly, extending a hand and placing his palm on the side of my neck. I felt his fingers twitch, and then a small sting against my throat. The scent of my own blood filled the room, and I could feel it trickling down my skin. His eyes zeroed in on that trickle, and he gritted out, "Dhampir blood is like a drug to us." He inched closer, licking his lips. My heart was beating frantically, making the blood gush out even faster. "It won't sustain us, but the high is…"

I arched my neck, allowing him greater access. I knew this was risky. This man was dangerous. He could drain me dry in seconds and I probably wouldn't be able to over-power him, but I wanted it. I was so tired of bottling up my desires and suppressing the monster inside. For a year, I'd been moving through my life like some kind of ghost. I'd been a shell of a woman, existing to take orders and bow down at a man's feet, but not anymore. I'd take the pleasure I wanted, and I'd relish the pain that came with it. Some-times, I craved the pain just as much—anything to feel again.

"Are you going to kill me, Merrick?" I asked, surprising myself. He paused, lips barely hovering over the incision on my neck.

"Do you want me to kill you, Serenity? You seem to crave it." Icy breath hit that trickle of blood, making me shiver. He was right—in a way, I did crave death. When I didn't answer, he added, "Killing you wouldn't do me much good, now would it?" His tongue lapped out once, licking up a single drop and causing my head to loll to the side as I stifled a moan. "Such a waste. No, I don't think killing you would do any of us any favors"

"So I'm supposed to be your prisoner indefinitely?"

"I think we both know you're no longer a prisoner. I can feel the strength coursing through your veins." His tongue swiped the incision. "You're strong, Serenity, stronger than we anticipated. If you agree to help us find the missing women, we'll free you from this cell."

My breath caught. Was he being serious? Just like that? All I had to do was agree to work with them and I'd be free? It would be so easy. But did I want to work with them? Could I? What would it mean for my mother? She was still at the mercy of Ryan Harker, and if I chose to ally myself with the Nocturne Coven, I would be making a very public statement for the world to see.

"Nothing to say to that?" he asked. I kept my mouth shut, unwilling to give him promises that I wasn't sure I could keep. "Good. Words are the last thing on my mind at the moment." His mouth latched onto my neck, and I felt the pull of blood leaving my veins.

Merrick moaned, the vibrations reverberating through my whole body. All thoughts of politics and scandal aside, I needed this vampire to touch me. Instinct was taking over. Instinct to bite, to feed. His pulse was racing, and I could hear the melodic sound of his heart beating like a drum. His hands skimmed up my thighs as blood ran down the front of my body. When deft fingers reached the apex, I felt his palm on my pussy, pressing down with the heel, causing me to roll my hips against it. His hand was massive and powerful. His whole body was a weapon, and it made me feel small and dainty, despite the power surging through me.

I wanted so badly to claw at his back or to grip him and pull him closer, but my hands were bound and I didn't feel like breaking the bonds. So I waited patiently as he undid his leather belt, pulling it free from the loops and letting it fall to the floor. He unbuttoned his pants with ease, pulling out his thick cock and giving it a single stroke. He was massive, and I instantly knew he was too thick for my fingers to wrap all the way around. I nearly snorted, thinking about how just days ago, I'd actually thought Carson's dick was impressive. He was a boy compared to the vampire in front of me.

My mouth watered for many reasons as he came forward, pulling my body flush with his. Our eyes caught and held as I spread my thighs wide on either side of his hips. He lifted me up, holding me steady as he placed me over his cock. I could feel the engorged tip at my entrance, and it was as if my body was physically pulsing for him.

He stopped and stilled for a moment, still holding my eyes as he said, "I don't know what it is about you, little dhampir, but I can't get you outta my head."

I nearly choked at that unexpected admission. I wasn't used to sincerity or honesty, so the blow and weight of those words hit me, struck me right in the chest as he eased his thick cock inside me. I couldn't help but moan as he slid in deep, saying, "Tell me why I can't get you out. Tell me why I see your face when I close my eyes..." He thrust once, deep and slow. My head fell back against the wall, and my eyes closed.

His thrusts began to speed up, and the cuffs chaining my wrists to the wall pulled taut. The only sounds in the room was the sound of metal clinking and the slaps of our skin as he fucked me. Our breathing was ragged, and my moans began to get louder. He was cursing, chanting, "Fuck, fuck, fuck..." over and over again.

Tilting my neck to the other side, I exposed my creamy skin to Merrick, and it didn't take him long to catch on to what I wanted. His teeth sank into my neck, all the while he never stopped pumping his cock into me. I was stretched so good, there were bloody tears in my eyes, and every so often he would still and grind his pelvis against my clit, eliciting a sharp hiss.

I couldn't take it anymore. The pleasure was too much and I needed to be free, so I yanked as hard as I could, breaking the chains off the wall. I raked my sharp nails down Merrick's back and felt blood trickle out of the wounds. For a human, these wounds would have been grave, but for a vampire, it was just considered foreplay. He ripped me from the wall, cock still buried inside me. I bounced on him, hands gripping his shoulders tight. He was incredibly strong and balanced me on his hips without a problem.

The skin around my eyes tightened, and I knew my eyes were changing colors to match his, the monster inside me coming out. I wasn't going to stop her this time. I felt my teeth elongate, aching for blood. Merrick pulled back to watch, and his gaze was feral at the sight of my vampire half. I was done holding back. Bringing my mouth down on his shoulder, I pierced his skin with my fangs, immediately feeling his hot, thick blood fill my mouth, dribbling down the side of my mouth and down his torso. He moaned, cock hardening inside me, and I immediately felt thick spurts of cum filling me up.

I'd heard before that biting between vampires was like an aphrodisiac. It wasn't done very often, but I'd heard rumors. His blood tasted like heaven, just as I remembered with Atlas the other day, and I wanted to gorge myself on it. Merrick moaned as I sucked, taking my fill, and he kept me bouncing on his dick as he came hard. The muscles in his arms bunched, hardening like steel, and I felt his fingers flexing as he held my hips tight.

Warmth built inside me as my eyes rolled back, and waves of pleasure filled me up, spreading through me like electricity. I'd never come this hard in my entire life, and I honestly never knew it could be this good. My orgasm lasted around thirty long seconds, easily tapering into a vibrating pulse as we slowed down. He held me against his slightly shivering body, and I removed my lips from his neck.

When I pulled back, I watched trickles of his blood flow over his muscular pecs, dripping down his torso. It took me a moment to realize he was watching my face, eyes glossed over in the aftershock of pleasure. "Shit, lass," he groaned, dick twitching again inside me.

I smiled, bending forward and running my tongue along the puncture wounds on his shoulder. A shiver rolled over him, and I watched in fascination as his wound knitted back together.

He was smiling when I looked back at him and said, "How'd ya know to do that?"

I frowned, glancing again from the now healed wound and then back to him. "I have no idea," I answered honestly. "Just kind of...felt right?"

He smiled wider, looking extremely satisfied with himself. With barely any effort, Merrick lifted me off his cock, and I groaned at the sensation, lamenting the loss of contact almost immediately. He set me on my feet, but I decided standing no longer sounded like much fun. I let myself topple to the padded floor and heard Merrick chuckle before he joined me. He tucked himself back into his pants and sat with his back resting against the wall.

I rolled onto my back, staring at the ceiling, not caring in the slightest that I was still covered in cooling blood. My body felt sated for the first time in forever. I felt a sense of completeness that I hadn't known was possible and wondered why the fuck I'd waited so long to give in to my true nature.

"Merrick?' I asked, eyes growing heavy as my head lolled to the side. Exhaustion was creeping over me quickly, and I knew I didn't have long.

"Yes?" he asked with a smile in his deep voice. It was nice to hear the change finally. It'd been so long since I'd heard something comforting.

"Are you going to kill me?" I whispered. I felt him go still. I didn't know how I knew it, but it was like I was attuned to his mood all of a sudden and I could feel how very tense he'd gone. I was seconds away from oblivion as I mumbled, "It's okay if you are...but...can you do me a favor?" He was silent, not moving a muscle, so I added, "Make it fast if you can. I think I'm tired of hurting..."

Darkness encroached on my vision as I shut my eyelids, ready to let the sleep take me away. I was so fucking tired, I wanted to hibernate for the next year. At least I was stated and warm. At least my veins didn't burn for what I denied them.

Right before sleep took me for good, I heard Merrick whisper softly and somberly, "No, lass, I don't think I'll be killin ya."

CHAPTER 13
FAUST

*U*nder the cover of night, Atlas and I left the mansion, taking one of the lower level tunnels that led out of the city. It was a ghost town in the Nocturne District, and we could've taken the streets, but these days, it was just too risky.

On the same level as the cell where we held Serenity, there was a series of tunnels built back before Noc City could even be called a city. The mansion had stood the test of time since the early eighteen hundreds, and we knew these passages like the back of our hands. It was a cold night, but the crisp air hit me like a refreshing wave. I needed the slap in the face. After being in a room with Serenity earlier, tied up with the scent of her blood still permeating the small space, it was all I could do not to rip into her throat and take what I wanted...and more.

I'd never been close with a dhampir, save for Loxley, Atlas' sister. She was a sister to the three of us, and I never once thought of her in such a way. But Serenity Harker...she was a different story. I tried to shake her off. The moment we met in her family's limousine, it had been like a blow to the face. The woman was an angel in every sense of the word. I'd seen her on TV of course, but the cameras didn't do her justice. She was perfect, flawless and... *No.* I shook my head for the millionth time as we sped through the tunnels, listening for anything amiss. I refused to think of her as anything but our prisoner.

We needed the information she had locked away inside that stubborn, prissy princess brain. She claimed to have no knowledge of what Dr. Bellamy and Senator Harker were up to, and to be honest, I was beginning to believe her. I no longer thought she was the insider we mistook her for, but rather an unwilling pawn in the senator's dangerous game. Still, it didn't mean she wasn't complicit in his rhetoric. She could have told him to fuck off with his blatant racism and left the way her cousin had. But she was weak, fickle, just like I suspected. There was still a chance she'd seen something she wasn't supposed to see, and we couldn't take the chance of letting her loose just yet. Besides, Atlas had another idea up his mischievous sleeves, and the girl's cooperation would prove to be vital.

Everything hinged on Serenity's cooperation. We needed to find the location of these testing facilities and liberate our people. All those females were wasting away at the hands of the humans...if they were still alive to waste away. There was no telling what was being done to them. I felt sick every time I thought about that wolf turning up human and dead on Blood Moon territory. Her veins had been engorged and filled with some kind of drug that caused her wolf DNA to recede and disappear altogether. It was unnatural, sick, and savage, and it needed to be stopped before we lost more darklings.

We'd thought this situation would go a lot smoother—

planting ourselves in the senator's household close to his daughter. We were supposed to follow her for weeks, studying her patterns, watching who she spoke to. We'd even gone so far as to purchase months worth of daylight potion from Bastian, our black market warlock contact. The stuff was vile, but it did the trick, changing not only our scent, but our tolerance to the sunlight and curbing our cravings. It was supposed to be the long game, until that fucking boyfriend of hers fucked it all up. My blood still boiled thinking about Carson Badgeley. I knew he was directly involved in the disappearances the moment he displayed his own girlfriend like chattel for the eyes of his colleagues. They way he'd stared at her with such revulsion and yet utter curiosity and lust had me imagining how good it would feel to spike his head on the city walls.

It was the first moment I'd had second thoughts about our plan. It was the first instance where doubt began to creep in, and I'd wondered if we had it all wrong and Serenity Harker was just another victim of her father's tyranny. But she'd taken any decision right out of our hands. I remembered the feeling of my heart in my throat as we drove on to the bridge, watching her white hair blowing in the wind as she stared down at the crashing waves. I knew what she was planning immediately, and I'd moved before I could tell myself to just let her make the choice for herself. I'd crashed into her hard and dragged her ass to the van, shoving a burlap sack over her head before she could see my face. It was the only thing I could think to do with our limited time.

Shortly after, the senator's helicopters and the city patrol had scoured Noc City. Merrick and I checked in periodically, still pretending to search for her. There had been witnesses on the bridge, reports of a blonde-haired girl leaping from the bridge. Naturally, many assumed she'd jumped to her death, but nothing had been confirmed until we showed that video in the city center. Even now, we were paying for it. Human protesters had been flooding the streets, demanding we free the girl. But they weren't just at our gates. Every coven in the city had come under fire since Senator Harker refused to make any public declarations, as well as the witches and warlocks. Darklings were guilty by association, and the humans were ready to be judge and jury. The senator knew we had her, but the public didn't.

Darklings rights activists matched the protester's fury every time, humans and darklings clashing head to head in the streets of Noc City for days. It was getting ugly, and the media was making it worse. Because of that, we'd been relegated to sneaking around through the tunnels, trying to leave the city without issue. We had a meeting with August, Alpha of the Blood Moon Pack in less than an hour. I wasn't looking forward to facing him after what had happened to those Blood Moon pups, but he deserved the respect of this meeting and the knowledge that this would not go unpunished.

August was a force to be reckoned with. He was ancient and wild, but he was a good man in my opinion, a good wolf. A warrior through and through. Legends of August and his battles ran deep through the darkling communities, and he was treated as a sort of mythical figure. I'd known him for years, as had Atlas and Merrick, but the shifter alpha still remained somewhat of a recluse. He and his wolves very rarely ventured into the city. He attended council meetings to respect the Coexist Doctrine, but that was the bare minimum. For the most part, the shifters kept to themselves out in the wilds surrounding the walled city.

I was right on Atlas' heels as we reached the entrance to

the tunnels. The moonlight lit the way and bathed us in pale white as we emerged. We didn't bother to stop, even with the sound of helicopters flying in the distance and the low hum of a thousand voices rising from the inner city. Noc City was a battleground, but it was only just beginning. Soon, the violence would begin, and it would be a blood-bath. Humans fought with their guns, while darklings ripped, clawed, and maimed. Still, I didn't regret provoking the senator. It was bound to happen eventually, and we were so close to cracking him.

We raced through the trees. The wildlands that surrounded the walled city were dense, shadowed, and rolling with thick fog. Howls could be heard in the distance, and we followed their chorus. The border to the Blood Moon territory clashed with the RedWood wolves extremely close to the walls. I hoped we wouldn't have to deal with a skirmish between packs tonight, as I just didn't have the energy for it.

After twenty minutes, I smelled the wolves. We came to a stop in a small clearing surrounded by tall trees, with small slivers of moonlight peeking through. I could hear the thudding of paws on packed earth and the heavy, melodic breathing of the wolves as they ran. I glanced at Atlas, and he met my eyes, mouth in a tight line. Not a hair was out of place and his suit was in impeccable shape, even after our mad dash out here. His eyes glowed tonight, and there was a harshness to the set of his jaw I didn't like. I was usually the grumpy bastard around here, but I could tell that all of this shit was weighing him down. I could also tell he was eager to get back to Serenity. His attachment to the little dhampir was becoming more apparent every day.

A few moments later, a little over ten wolf shifters emerged from the foliage, stalking forward on silent feet.

You could always tell the difference between shifters and wild animals, mainly in the way that they moved. There was still something decidedly human in their stillness and the clarity in their gaze. There was a time, centuries ago, where we'd been mortal enemies. I couldn't even count on one hand the number of battles I'd fought against wolf packs around the world. But not any more. We'd come to a truce when the humans rebelled against us. Darklings had no choice but to put aside our differences and stand together against a common enemy.

The shifters remained in wolf form, save for two men. They walked out of the tree line, stark naked. Both of them were nearly seven feet tall and built like tanks. August was on the right, and his cousin and right-hand wolf, Gareth, was on the left. Gareth hung back slightly as August approached. He was a sight to behold, objectively. I wasn't one to shy away from admitting to another man's beauty. He was massive, tanned skin decorated in silver battle scars that reminded me a lot of the ones I'd seen on Serenity's skin. Some wounds were just too deep to heal. His hair hung just past his shoulders in dark golden waves that matched his thick beard, and his eyes were golden, glimmering in the bright moonlight. There was nothing human about August.

"Do you have wolves in the city?" Atlas asked, not bothering with pleasantries.

August folded his massive arms over his chest, not caring in the slightest that he was bare ass naked. Wolves were feral creatures, and human sensibilities meant nothing to them. "Only scouts, but they're holding back, sticking to the rooftops for now." His voice was so low, it sounded like a growl, even in his human form. There was no question he was the alpha.

Atlas nodded. "Good. I'd like to extend my apologies for

the pups that were killed in the city center," he said sincerely. My gut twisted just remembering it and the feeling of helplessness at being forced to watch it happen. "I'm sorry we couldn't intervene."

August blinked, and for a moment, I wondered if this was about to go south. But instead, he nodded curtly and said, "Appreciated."

I cleared my throat, stepping forward, and watched as August turned his focused attention on me and asked before I could speak, "The girl. Have you...coaxed any information from her?" He sneered as he uttered the word *coaxed*. We all knew the manner with which we were willing to behave for answers. His gaze, however, held no judgement.

I spoke first, Atlas not caring that I was technically his second and not the coven leader. "Not as much as we hoped. She knows nothing about the facilities, and so far, I've detected nothing but truth." August's eyes darkened at that as I added, "But there may be other ways with which we can use her to our advantage."

"Explain," he barked, sounding more on edge than before. Gareth was shifting on his feet behind him, probably salivating for the order to storm the city and slaughter the humans.

"Before we took her, she'd been in the process of being sold to colleagues of the senator. We witnessed the exchange firsthand, and it sped up the timeline." I clenched my jaw at the memory of that horrible fucking night. "The girl has suffered greatly, and we only just found out that she is a dhampir, not a human like we thought." I kept my face neutral as August let his emotionless mask slip for a second, eyes widening before shuttering once more. I kept going. "Seems Elodie Harker was a naughty little human twenty-four years ago. We know for a fact that the senator wants to keep the fact that he raised the bastard daughter of a vampire under his own roof and then proceeded to hide it from the public for a year after the assassination of his son a secret. We can use this against him, along with the fact that Serenity seems to loathe Ryan Harker even more than we do."

"Loathe him why?" This came from Gareth, who took a step closer. August said nothing, letting his second ask his questions, probably just as interested in the answer.

Atlas and I exchanged wary glances. I didn't feel like we should hash this all out at this particular moment, but if we wanted to keep August and his wolves on our side, we needed to be transparent. I said, "Her body is scarred. She's been beaten pretty badly it seems, most likely over the course of the last year after the senator found out about her mother's infidelity. But she starved herself of blood and never properly healed or transitioned. We haven't gotten much out of her in the way of details, but it's pretty clear who's responsible for those scars. I believe she has every reason to hate the man, as any darkling does."

Something violent passed in August's gaze the moment I mentioned her scars. I watched his shoulders tense even more than they already were, and Gareth's eyes were now glued to his alpha. Some of the wolves behind them were shifting uncomfortably. Wolves were pack animals, and they took the care of their females very seriously. Serenity wasn't one of them, but I could see how uncomfortable they were with this unexpected revelation. I'd felt the same way the first time I realized something wasn't right in the Harker household—the first time I'd seen the deadness in Serenity's deep brown eyes. The world was under the impression that she was a perfect little angel, smiling next to her doting father, running charity events and raising money against people like me. But I was beginning to realize that was far from the reality. I still wasn't sure how to feel about it.

After a few long moments, August finally spoke. "We're taking three days to bury and mourn our pups. Three days uninterrupted, as per pack law." I clenched my jaw, but he continued, saying, "After that, my wolves are at your disposal. I'd like to meet this Serenity Harker for myself. If we deem her unfit, she will be disposed of in a public manner."

A hiss built inside me, but a sharp look from Atlas had me holding it in. "Disposed of how?" he asked.

August looked wicked as he said, "It's not my job to decide, but yours. If we find out she knows more than she's letting on or that she plans to betray us, then there will be no mercy for her, dhampir or not."

He was dead serious, I could see it in his eyes. With two pups slaughtered in the streets at the hands of Harker's supporters and a handful of missing female wolves, there was no more room for mercy.

"Fair enough," Atlas said, though I could hear the obvious strain in his voice. "We'll give you three days to mourn your pups. We'll send an emissary to pay our respects at sundown."

August nodded, already turning his back on us. That was just how the shifter alpha operated—curt and to the point. Nobody had ever accused him of being friendly. But before he had a chance to shift back into his wolf form, I called out one last time. "One more thing," I said. August stilled and turned around to meet my gaze. He waited, so I added with stiff shoulders and a rock in my gut, "Another female has gone missing. My contacts told me only an hour ago." August's eyes darkened even more, burning molten amber. "This one's a human. Her name is Beatrix Castwell, and she's Serenity's closest cousin."

The words were hollow, echoing off the surrounding woods. I watched August take in the information and nod solemnly before turning around once more and shifting seamlessly into a midnight black wolf. Howls filled the night as his pack followed behind him, echoing through the forest. More howls met theirs in the distance, and so Atlas and I took that as our cue to leave. Now came the hard part —letting our captive know that her beloved cousin was the senator's newest victim.

CHAPTER 14
SERENITY

I woke from a dreamless sleep to the feeling of being watched. My arms were unbound, and I was no longer chained to the floor. It all came back to me in a flash of memory. Merrick was nowhere to be found. It was just me and this shredded black night dress.

The feeling of being watched persisted, so I looked up towards the dark glass window, knowing there was someone standing just on the other side. The more blood I was able to consume, the more heightened my senses became. It was strange, hearing and sensing things I was once blind to. My body ached, but it was a good kind of ache, one that confirmed the fact that the previous night hadn't just been some kind of fever dream.

I glanced back to the wall where the broken cuffs dangled from useless chains, vividly recalling the violence with which Merrick fucked me. I hadn't expected to enjoy it as much as I had. I'd assumed, at first, that it was just the bloodlust talking, that it was overriding my senses and causing me to crave other things. But I didn't think that was the case. Being with Merrick was different from my encounters with Carson. Though he was a vampire, and possibly centuries old if not more, I felt a connection I hadn't ever felt with my boyfriend. I could even say the same thing about my first encounter with Atlas back at Rue. We hadn't gone as far as I'd craved at the time, but even those short moments had felt so different.

I found myself reevaluating my time here and wondering if I'd be better off joining their cause. Realistically, I could never go back home, and I wasn't sure I would, even if they let me. I'd been ready to kill myself just to get away from Ryan and Carson, so would it really be so bad to fight for the other team? I supposed one could call it Stockholm syndrome, but I didn't think that was it. This world was fucked up, and people were forced to choose sides. Up until now, I'd never been forced to make that choice for myself, but perhaps it was time.

I jumped when a section of the wall behind me slid open. The lights remained on this time, and in walked the only one of the three I had yet to see face to face. Faust stepped into the red light of the dark room, and it glinted off the barbell piercing through his eyebrow. His dark blond hair was combed to the side, and his jaw was clean shaven. I'd almost forgotten what a handsome bastard he was, even when I thought he was just my goon. The entrance slid closed, trapping the two of us in here together.

We stared at each other for more than a few heavy heartbeats before he cleared his throat. "Shower time," he said gruffly. I blinked. And then I blinked again. He lifted one brow and said, "Now, unless you feel like sitting around in your own filth for the next twenty-four hours." His nose wrinkled as he looked me up and down.

I got to my feet slowly, hoping my dress managed to stay

together. "Are we still pretending like I'm a prisoner?" I asked dryly.

His face didn't change. There was no wry smirk or even a small flash of humor in his dark brown eyes, just emotionless emptiness. It made me wonder what kind of shit this man had seen in his life to utterly erase any sort of personality. I ignored his lack of response and followed him to the door. Apparently, they were no longer bothering with the cloak and dagger tactics. Still, I went along with it, realizing I did need a shower. I probably smelled pretty ripe after what Merrick and I had gotten up to the night before. I wondered if Faust was aware.

The door slid open again, and a waft of what I could only describe as fresh night air caressed my skin. It was tinged sweet with the smell of pine, and through the darkness of the hallways, I could see small dustmotes floating around the empty space. Before I had the chance to step out, Faust suddenly whipped around, pressing against me until I was flush with the doorframe.

"You make one wrong move, and I will not hesitate to take you out, you hear me? I'm infinitely stronger than you are, dhampir. You run, and I will catch you. You fight me, and I will win, got it?" His eyes bore into mine, and his breath hit my face in short bursts. This close up, I could still see the bright crimson lurking just underneath the brown.

"You got it, boss," I said cheekily with a small, taunting wink. And I did get it. I was pretty resolved by now that I would be helping them in any way I could, if only to get out of that fucking padded room.

We stared at each other, and for a split second, I watched in disbelief as his cold eyes flickered to my lips before he looked away. He thought he was slick, but I'd seen it. I smiled at the back of his head as he led me farther down the hallway, presumably towards the same bathroom I'd gone to before for my last shower.

The room was already filled with steam when we entered, and I had to blink furiously against the stark white light of the sterile tiles. The shower heads were already running, making me wonder if Faust had come in here beforehand to do it. The thought made me smirk. They were trying so hard to be pricks, but they failed to realize that I'd dealt with much worse over the years. This was play-time as far as I was concerned.

I didn't wait for instructions, fully understanding how the mechanics of a shower worked. I stripped out of the ripped nightie and let it fall to the floor as Faust kept his brown eyes on me. I felt gross and probably smelled even worse. The moment I stepped under the hot spray, I tilted back my head and let loose a long sigh of contentment. I could still feel his eyes boring a hole into my back and wondered why this was part of protocol. Surely I could manage to shower in private without thwarting their grand plans. If they thought a little nudity would scare me off, they were severely underestimating me. There was a difference between being naked of your own accord and being forced. I'd learned that difference well over the last few years. Consent was the name of the game.

As I washed, I thought about my predicament and what I knew I needed to do. I'd come to the conclusion that I had to stop sitting on my thumbs and actually do something for once in my life. I'd been standing idly behind the senator like a good little bitch for too long, always afraid for my own safety. I'd been selfish, and that had become clearer the longer I stayed here. I thought about Trix and the sacrifices she'd made in the name of what she believed in. She'd lost family, friends, and her reputation because she believed in something with her whole heart. I could probably stand to be a little more like my cousin. These men had every right to distrust me. It wasn't like I was a child.

Clearing my throat to break the awkward silence, I didn't bother to turn around as I said, "Those wolf pups..." There was silence behind me. I knew he was still there, just watching me, so I continued, "Did they really die because of me?"

Silence again, and I thought he might choose to ignore the question outright. It would probably serve me right. I'd been thinking about those wolves. In my dreams last night, I'd seen them—the shifters who sometimes turned up to hear my father speak. I'd seen them there and always wondered why they bothered to listen to a man who hated them. I was beginning to understand the logic. It was good to know your enemy, to study them. Perhaps that was where the humans got it wrong. Humans thought they were superior in every way to the animals. That was all darklings were to them.

"Yes," Faust said suddenly. My shoulders stiffened, and the water began to grow cold. I couldn't turn and face him just yet. "Is that what you wanted to hear?"

Bitterness rolled through me at his condescending tone. Snapping my head around, I met his eyes, frown to frown. He was leaning against the basin with his tattooed arms folded over his chest. My eyes flickered over him, realizing I'd had no idea he was covered in ink. Every time I'd seen him, he'd been wearing either a suit or a long-sleeved hoodie. The ink suited him, I decided. Suited all of them, actually.

"How?" I asked simply.

A muscle ticked in his square jaw. "They were executed on the steps of city hall after we leaked footage of your capture to the public." There was zero remorse in his tone, but as I sucked in a sharp breath, I could have sworn I saw a hint of sadness there. It was gone in a flash. "That's what your people do, Serenity. That's how they operate. They call us the animals, but they're the real savages."

"You say that as if I pulled the trigger myself," I gritted, shutting off the water. The room was pleasantly warm, and the steam was thick, making it harder to see Faust.

"Didn't you though?" he asked, standing taller and squaring his broad shoulders. "You were fine with it before you found out you were one of the monsters. What makes things so different now?" Dropping his arms, he took a step forward. "You think you're one of us, but you'll never understand what it's like to be persecuted for existing, to be hunted in the streets and executed without justice. You'll never get it because for nearly thirty years, you watched and kept silent while other people suffered. At least your brother paid the price."

My body stiffened, my blood running colder than ice. "You don't get to talk about my brother." My voice came out low and threatening. I didn't sound quite like myself. Dripping hair and all, I stepped closer, feeling my nails and teeth lengthen as anger filled me up. "Say what you want about me, but you leave the dead out of this." His frown never wavered, but there was something in his eyes this time...a flash of something that looked like regret, but I couldn't say for sure.

"You're not in any position to make demands, little dhampir," Faust sneered, glaring at me like I was filth. Like I was nothing more than one of the humans he hated so much.

"You think I haven't suffered?" I asked, cocking my head to the side and coming closer. I was vaguely aware of the sound of footsteps down the hall, and then a whoosh of cold air flowed into the bathroom as the door opened. Still, my gaze remained on Faust, even as I scented both Merrick and Atlas entering the room.

"No." That single word was like a snap in the tense silence.

I nearly smiled as I said, "I might not know what it's like to be hunted, but don't you ever tell me I don't know suffering." I was right up in his face now, knowing the others were watching warily. Faust didn't move a muscle. "Have you ever been beaten so badly that your bones poked out from your skin, Faust? Little broken white shards jutting out from bloody stumps that take weeks to regrow? Have you had your teeth knocked out and spilled over the expensive flooring of your own home while your bodyguards averted their eyes, or had to stand there while your father made your own mother whip you bloody, until you couldn't see or hear anymore?" I watched him swallow, still frowning down at me, but I wasn't finished. I could feel hot tears rolling down my face, and I knew they were crimson, coating my pale cheeks.

"Have you been forced to let a sadist fuck you night after night until you were bleeding and vomiting in the shower because he thought he owned you? Were you paraded like chattel for powerful men to ogle and poke and judge? Did you—" I choked, stumbling over the memories as they hit me all at once. "Do you have any idea what it's like to have the man you thought was your father for twenty-four years promise to fuck you so hard you couldn't stand? To feel his hands on your skin and his fingers creeping in places no father should ever see? Do you know what that's like, you fucking prick!? Because I know what that's like! I know how it feels to have no other way out, to crave the silence and the

189

goddamn freedom of jumping off that bridge. I know what suffering is, and if you can't understand that, then fuck you!"

I hadn't realized I was pressing him onto the basin, but his arms were uncrossed, hands balled into fists at his side. I watched his jaw tighten and his breathing pick up. Faust stared at me, not bothering to open his big stupid mouth. I guessed he had nothing to say to that. *Asshole.* Before I could say anything else, there was a hand on my shoulder. I stiffened, and Faust's eyes flickered to whoever was behind me and glared.

"C'mon, lass, let's get ya dressed," Merrick said softly. He tugged me backwards gently, but I shrugged off his hand.

"I can do it myself," I snapped. Merrick frowned but backed away as I mumbled a few profanities under my breath.

"Yeah, Merrick, she can put her own clothes on," Faust said suddenly, sounding incredibly bitter, but I assumed that was just the norm for him at this point, until he added, "Or is that your job, too, now that she's letting you take them off?"

Sucking in a breath, I whipped back around, pinning him with a glare as Merrick stepped up, squaring his shoulders. "Fuck you, man," he snapped.

Faust smiled bitterly. "If I ask nicely, maybe Serenity will do just that."

"What the hell are you talking about?" Atlas asked, eyes bouncing between the three of us. "Merrick, what happened?" Merrick was quiet, jaw clenched as he and Faust seemed to have a glare off, so Atlas asked again, "Merrick, I asked you a question. Did you—" He coughed, eyes flickering to me for a split second. "Did you fuck our prisoner?"

I snorted. "Oh that's rich coming from you." All eyes

turned to me as I shook my head at Atlas. I made my way over to the standing coat rack and pulled the clothing from the hook while they all watched. At least this time there were some undergarments, a pair of jeans that surprisingly fit, and a black tank. "Don't pretend to be all high and mighty, coven leader, as if you didn't try the same thing in this very room."

Atlas choked, eyes going wide before his face settled into a deep frown. My smile was fading at the bewildered and confused look on his face. "What the hell are you talking about?"

"You can cut the shit, Atlas," I sneered.

"I'm being serious," he insisted. "I haven't touched you like that since Rue."

What? That wasn't true. I remembered very clearly. I could still feel the way those gloved fingers played over my clit and how I came undone so quickly in this very spot. It hadn't been Merrick. The man had spoken in an American accent, but I thought... "That makes no sense." I shook my head back and forth. "We...in here...you," I stuttered, puzzling it out but to no avail.

Booming laughter had me whipping back around to face the other two. Merrick had tears in his eyes as he threw his head back in laughter, all the while Faust just stood there once again, jaw clenched so hard I thought his teeth might break, with his arms over his chest. "Oh, shit!" Merrick practically wheezed. "I don't wanna hear another fuckin' word from you, ya dumb shit."

I frowned at the two of them, seemingly lost, until it fucking hit me. I met Faust's eyes as fury rolled through me. "Oh my god, that was you?!" *Holy shit...* This whole time, it was Faust?! My mind was spinning. I'd thought it had been Atlas making me feel those things, touching me with expert ease, but it was Faust all along. The man who proclaimed to loathe me, who would probably rather see me thrown to the streets than join their coven.

I lunged for Faust, planning on tackling the big bastard to the ground, but before I could take a single step, there was a massive boom that shook the building. The walls vibrated, and Merrick reached for me, trying to steady the two of us as I slipped on the tile. Another two booms rocked the room. "What the hell was that?!"

"Come on!" Atlas shouted, already prying the door off its hinges.

"What's happening?" I asked as we rushed out into the dark hallway. Merrick had a hold of my arm and hauled me along so fast that the walls blurred around us.

Red lights were flashing, and a blaring alarm sounded overhead. Dirt rained down on our heads as thuds reverberated through the tunnels. "We're being attacked," Merrick gritted out as we turned corner after corner. I had no idea how far underground we were, and it was too hard to get any sense of direction in this fucking labrynth.

"By who?" I asked breathlessly. Another jolt had us gripping the walls as the tunnel shook.

"Who the fuck do you think?!" Faust tossed over his shoulder. I glared at him and bit back a retort. "We need to get to the surface now before the tunnels come down. It sounds like they're using more than just pipe bombs."

"You think the human protesters are doing this?" I asked, leaping over a pile of fallen concrete. I could barely see now as a cloud of dust filled the tight space. "This seems like more than that. How far underground are we?" There was no answer. We just kept running, so I demanded one. "Answer me, assholes!"

"Three floors!" Atlas shouted back finally. The elevators

we passed were a no go, so we had to head for any available staircase. "Serenity, they're here for you," he said. "You're going to let them take you."

"Are you crazy?" I shook off Merrick's tight grip, trying to keep my balance. "What the fuck was all this for then? You expect me to go back to him? Fuck you, Atlas!"

"We were going to bring it up anyway—Left!" he shouted, and we took our immediate left as rubble fell over us. "If you really want to help us, you can do it better from the inside."

"You can't force me to—" I coughed as I inhaled dust. I was running out of steam, and my eyes were stinging as we fought through. "I'm not going back there..."

Faust let Atlas overtake him, turning back to me. He gripped my arm tight and hauled me next to him as I fought to pull away. "You'll do what you're fucking told, princess."

"Or what?" I snapped. There was nothing more they could do to me. I'd already seen the worst of it.

"Or your cousin might be the next woman to turn up dead."

I skidded to a dead stop, the world still shaking around us. "What the fuck did you just say to me? Are you threatening Trix?" My fangs were extended, and I could feel my nails sharpening into points. "If you touch her—"

"You'd know this shit if you just cooperated instead of acting like a whiny little princess. Your cousin has gone missing. The first human woman we know of. We were going to tell you later, but I guess now's as good a time as any. Get your shit together, Serenity. There are more important things going on, and we can't always cater to your fragile feelings." His face was in mine, and his eyes blazed red. His words were like a blow to the face, but...he was right.

My heart was in my throat as I thought of Trix in the hands of Dr. Bellamy. Whatever these facilities were...whatever they were doing with this crazy drug couldn't mean anything good for her. *Fuck*... Trix was a human. Was if my fault they'd taken her? To provoke me? I didn't think I could live with myself if they hurt her because of me.

"We don't have time for this!" Atlas shouted from up ahead. He was right too—we didn't have time for this. "Come on!"

Faust turned around and continued down the tunnel, but before I could follow, the tunnel rocked again as a massive explosion sounded overhead. The ceiling collapsed between us, raining down like a waterfall of concrete, wood, and dirt. I screamed, and I could hear the sounds of the guys shouting frantically. The more concrete that fell, the quieter their voices became, until I couldn't hear anything but the sound of ground crumbling.

Turning back, I ran away from the falling ceiling, careening around corners, even though I had no idea where I was going. It was only a matter of time until whatever building was overhead came down on top of us. I just hoped the guys wouldn't waste their time trying to get to me. I hoped they'd be smart enough to get out in time. I decided trying to get back to them wouldn't work, and I could feel a waft of air blowing in from down the tunnel. I smelled pine on the air and followed it, the first I'd sensed since I was taken from the bridge.

I must have been trapped on the right side of the rubble, because through the smoke and debris, I could barely make out the soft white light of what I assumed was either a streetlight or the moon, so I followed it. Coughing and inhaling the dust made my lungs burn, and my eyes dripped crimson tears as I felt like I was blinking against sandpaper.

As I stepped over fallen concrete, there was another boom from overhead, and I fell against the tunnel wall, crashing into a busted pipe that tore through the skin on my arm. I screamed at the sudden, burning pain, but I kept on going. I'd heal quicker than normal, thanks to my recent gorge on blood, but it still hurt like a bitch.

After shoving aside cinder blocks and leaping over toppled walls and doors, that sliver of light became more clear. There was a pile of rubble leading up a steep incline, and at the top was a hole the size of a doggy door. Through it, I could see the night sky and a few trees. My heart soared, but bitterness squirmed in my gut, wondering if I should go back for the guys. They were still trapped down there if there wasn't another way out on the other side.

I didn't think I could live with myself if I left them. They'd kidnapped me, lied to me, and put me through hell, but...I just couldn't do it. I couldn't leave them. I'd already made the decision to help their cause, and I wasn't about to leave them for dead. Turning away from my way out, I fought back down the pile, calling out each of their names as loud as I could, not knowing if the sound would even travel over the booms and shakes of the building's foundation. There was a war raging overhead, and I already dreaded seeing the aftermath once I got to the surface. My gut clenched, realizing I'd been the catalyst for so much destruction.

I was halfway down the debris pile when another boom shook the tunnels, sending the ceiling crashing in. It fell between myself and the way I needed to go to get back to the guys. I scrambled backwards just as a series of pipes came down overhead, water rushing out fast enough to knock me over. I turned, climbing for my life up that incline, desperately crawling to get to the entrance. I slipped and fell every few feet, but I was moving faster than I'd ever moved before, faster than I could as a human.

With a strength I didn't know I had, I finally reached the top, kicking out against the narrow hole until I was bashing cinder blocks outwards. I'd created a larger hole, gabbing onto a metal bar overhead and hauling myself out into the night. Crisp air hit my face, and I struggled to inhale deep lungfuls of air, hacking up powdered concrete and smoke.

The danger wasn't gone quite yet, though. It was chaos at the surface. Helicopters were circling overhead, the symbol of the Noc City police on the sides. Their search-lights roved the surrounding woods, and I realized quickly that these tunnels led me outside of the city walls. I'd never left the city alone before, and even then, it had always been in a private jet. The woods around me were thick and wild and too dark to see much, in the slivers of moonlight peeking through.

I knew I needed to get away before any ground patrol could find me. If Atlas was right and they were really here for me, there was no telling what would happen once I was caught. I'd probably be turned back over to Ryan and prob-ably Dr. Bellamy. I wasn't in any shape to fight them off. So I ran farther into the woods, having no idea which way I needed to go. I just knew that the farther away from those helicopters I got, the better.

Trees passed me in a blur, and I noticed belatedly that I was limping slightly, despite how fast I was able to run. Pain shot up my leg, and I realized I must have been injured worse than I'd originally thought. Blood gushed down my arm where that metal had torn through the skin, but I couldn't stop to mend it. I just kept on running, following the moon as it watched me from overhead.

After about twenty minutes of running, I slowed,

running out of breath, my arm and my leg throbbing. I bent over at the waist, dry heaving as I fought to catch my breath. I blinked through the tears and pain, shivering as the adrenaline waned. It took too long for me to realize that something wasn't quite right...

The woods had gone quiet and still. Insects had stopped chirping, and I suddenly felt as if I was being watched. I didn't know how I knew it, but there was a prickle of awareness that caused my skin to pebble. I sniffed, scenting the air in case it was one of the guys, who'd hopefully managed to get out of the tunnels. But...I was wrong. I didn't smell vampire. I smelled wolves.

My heart lurched as I took off in a dead sprint. The next thing I knew, howls and snarls rent the air. I heard the thudding of paws behind me and knew the wolves were giving chase. I knew immediately that they were shifters and realized I was smack in the heart of shifter pack lands. I'd never been here before, but I'd heard stories as I grew up about the vicious wolf packs that fought with each other from time to time over who owned the land.

I thought of the wolf pups who'd been killed in the city a few days ago, and dread pooled in my gut. If these shifters knew who I was, there was no doubt in my mind that they'd be out for my blood, out for revenge. I raced on, running for my life as the wolves closed in behind me. Up ahead, I came to a small clearing of downed foliage, but I skidded to a stop before I could get through it.

Two massive wolves leapt from the shadows, and the hairs on their backs rose as their teeth glared in the moonlight. Eyes filled with fury and the instinct to hunt stared back at me, glowing blue and yellow in the darkness. I scrambled backwards, hitting a tree hard enough to knock the wind out of me. I glanced around, trying to find a way to escape, but all I found on every side of me were more wolves stalking closer.

I was stronger than ever before, but I knew I wasn't strong enough to take on a pack of shifters. I didn't stand a chance. This was it for me—the end of the road. I wondered how much of my body would be left for the authorities to find. I wondered what would happen to the city after my death. Many people would suffer, both humans and dark-lings alike. Fear and sadness filled me up at the thought of my legacy. I was the catalyst to one of the biggest race wars in history, and my panic and stupidity would be my down-fall. I cursed myself for the last time, finally coming to terms with my fate.

I stared into the eyes of a wolf with scarring that marred its face. He was missing an eye, and he looked like he was salivating over the hunt. Instead of fear, a wave of warmth rushed over me as he crept closer. I was surprised at the calmness inside me, like a blanket had shrouded me from the biting chill of the night. I was ready for this end, resigned to it. Numb to it. So I nodded to the scarred wolf, beckoning him to take his prize. He lunged for my throat, and my world went dark.

CHAPTER 15
AUGUST

I smelled her before I saw her. The sharp tang of blood was mixed with the unmistakable scent of female. I got off the phone with Atlas Nocturne the second it registered.

His frantic voice shouting from the other end of the line spurred me into action. The girl they held captive was gone, escaped in the dead of night as an attack on the Nocturne Coven house reduced it to rubble. We'd been anticipating such an attack, but it came sooner than we'd thought it would. Atlas and his men were frantic trying to find the missing woman after getting separated in their escape. I'd heard a lot about her over the last few days, and I wasn't too impressed. That sniveling little bitch had gotten two of my pack pups killed. Her family was a cancer on Noc City, her father a tyrant and her mother clearly a drunken, vacant fool.

Atlas, Faust, and Merrick, the three heads of the Nocturne Coven, were allies of a sort. I couldn't exactly call them friends, but I'd known Atlas since the early seventeen hundreds, when we'd arrived in New York for the first time. We'd held a tenuous truce between Blood Moon and Nocturne, watching each other's backs and allying against the human factions in the early twenty-twenties before the signing of the Coexist Doctrine. Merrick Nocturne was like a brother to the coven leader, a turned vampire who'd been left for dead during the Irish rebellion, and Faust...well, he was another story. I still wasn't too sure what the deal with him was exactly, but he'd joined up with Atlas in the nine-teen-twenties and never left. He was a brute of a man, cold and arrogant, but he was loyal to a fault and I could respect that.

They were convinced that Serenity Harker could help us locate the facilities the famous Dr. Bellmy ran under the patronage of Senator Ryan Harker. She was supposed to be the key to it all, and those vampire fools let her slip through their fingers. As much as I respected Atlas, he was becoming lax. Over the years, he'd grown much too comfortable in that posh, modernized city, away from his warrior roots and vulnerable to the humans. I'd done no such thing. The Blood Moon Pack held roots deep in battle forged settle-ments from Europe to the United States. We'd fought count-less wars with a revolving door of human dictators. Of course, back then, darklings were still a well preserved secret.

I raced through the trees, knowing my betas were close behind a little less than a half mile back. My right-hand wolf, Gareth, loped next to me, matching my pace. I sprinted in wolf form, feeling the biting wind sifting through my black fur. The trees were dense this far out into Blood Moon territory. We were located just outside of Noc City in a section of wild forest reserved for the two wolf packs that surrounded the settlement. The Blood Moon Pack held the northern end, while the RedWood Pack held the southern end. I kept my head on a swivel when we began to reach the border between packs. RedWood's alpha was a son of a bitch and would raise hell if one of my wolves encroached on his land.

I could smell that nearly floral, honey-like scent of the female. Human...but also not. She smelled surprisingly pleasant. Atlas had informed me that the girl was a dhampir, but I'd never been close to one myself. Wolves didn't associate much with the vamps or the humans, save for the young pups who headed into the cities to search out their mates. Mates would often be found among the humans, and together, they bore half-blood pups. It didn't matter much to me, a wolf was a wolf in any form, but I'd never found my mate. Over a thousand years of searching the world, and I was positive no such creature existed.

As we ran, the trees blurring on all sides, I scented someone else on the wind, and a low growl slipped from my snarling mouth. At the same time, Gareth let a snarl rip, and I glanced to the side, meeting his bright blue wolf eyes. I smelled the RedWood wolves close to the female, their scents mixing, and I could already smell the excitement emanating from them from here. Raising my head, I howled as loud as I could up towards the starry sky, and a split second later, I was met with a chorus of responding cries from my betas. It was a warning. They needed to be ready for a fight if the RedWood wolves were here to start some shit.

To the eye of a human, we'd be nothing more than a blur. As we broke through a small clearing through the tall trees, I could clearly make out a slender woman lying limply on the forest floor. She wore little to no clothes, save for a tiny black tank top and jeans that were ripped clean open, her pale skin soaked in clotting blood. Her long, snowy white hair was a twisted mess around her face and equally matted with crimson. As we neared, I could see no visible wounds on her body, but she would most likely have healed by now, given she was half-immortal.

Before we reached her, several large wolves leapt from the surrounding foliage, hackles raised and maws dripping with saliva. Their eyes were locked on both myself and Gareth, who slunk to my side, making sure he'd be ready to leap in front of his alpha if need be. I appreciated his protection, but I didn't need it. I'd been handling myself for a thousand years and hadn't fallen yet. By their scents, I could tell I wasn't dealing with the top brass. These were grunts, probably out on a hunt until they stumbled upon this helpless female. One of the deep brown wolves on my right kept glancing at her prone form, as if he planned to drag her off the moment we were distracted.

I knew their tricks and knew that as clever as they thought they were, I was a strategist and could see every one of their moves a mile away. The wolf at the front of the line lunged, going for my throat. I moved in a blur before he had a chance to snarl. My jaw clamped down into his fur, and I could feel the bones breaking as my mouth filled with hot, coppery blood. The wolf whined and went limp, prompting me to drop him to the dirt, dead in an instant.

The other wolves whined and halted their attack, glancing at one another, and I knew they were making a decision, wondering if it was worth their time to directly challenge the Alpha of Blood Moon. It would be foolish on their part. I'd been killing since the day I learned how to shift, and my name was legendary for a reason. Before the remaining wolves could come to a decision, my betas crashed through the trees and into the clearing. There were ten of them at my back now. If I could smile in wolf form, I would have. Instead, I stared the wolves down as they seemed to shrink back into themselves, obviously realizing they'd lost.

My wolves snarled and growled, forming a tight line next to me, a solid wall of death, and I could scent the new fear tinging the crisp forest air. One by one, the RedWood wolves started to retreat, taking off into the trees. One wolf remained and stared me down too long for a wolf with such a low ranking. I could scent that he wasn't a beta or anywhere even close to important in the hierarchy. He was scum. He had greyish fur with small patches where chunks had been ripped out in previous scraps. He was missing his right eye, and the other had a deep gash through it. An ugly son of a bitch, and scrawny, too. His claws were grown out to the point that they were breaking off in jagged points. Fucking mutt. After a too long minute, the wolf huffed and turned away, racing off into the trees. Though he was gone in seconds, I had a feeling we'd be seeing more of him very soon.

With the wolves gone, my men and I shifted back into our human forms with ease, naked as they day we were born. Nudity wasn't a big deal among wolves, as we spent half of our time as animals. As I got closer to the pale woman, I could make out her features a little easier. She couldn't have been any older than maybe twenty-five at the most. Her face, though covered in blood and patches of drying mud, was undeniably beautiful. She had a delicate bone structure and light freckles scattered across her nose. Her pale skin looked soft and supple, but what really made me pause were her fingernails. Underneath each nail was coated in thick, congealing blood, and not her own. Whatever had happened to her hadn't happened without a fight on her part.

Gareth spoke first. "Orders, Alpha?" He came up beside me, also studying the woman with a frown between his light blond brows.

I glanced behind me and said, "Cody and Ash, lift her and let's get her to Christophe. Once we know she's not dying, we'll figure out what to do with her. I'll put in the call to Atlas when we return." My two largest wolves immediately bent and lifted her into their arms.

In less than a heartbeat after they'd lifted her up, something weird filled my stomach—a feeling of unease that I had to swallow back and ignore. I must have made some noise of discomfort, because Gareth gave me a strange look. I shook my head, waving him off.

Together, we ran back through the Blood Moon territory, feeling more at ease the closer we got to our home. I was puzzled about the woman. These woods were thick, and she had to have been hauling ass to get this far out as fast as she did, especially if she encountered RedWood wolves on a hunt. I was honestly surprised she was still alive. I knew Atlas' property backed up against the border of Noc City and that there were multiple ways both in and out utilized for decades, unbeknownst to the humans.

I found myself glancing towards the girl in the arms of my packmates. Her long silvery white hair practically glowed in the moonlight, and her skin was nearly pearlescent. I'd seen her image on television a handful of times, as most had. She was a celebrity in the realest sense, but I'd never given her a second thought. The Angel of Noc City, they called her. Precious and delicate... Well, we'd put that to the test here very soon. That she'd been discovered to be half-immortal was jarring. Senator Harker was indeed keeping more secrets than we'd originally thought.

In the distance, our village came into view. Small cabins were scattered around in a circle, which surrounded the pack house in the center. The massive house was where myself and my family lived and where the pack held important meetings and events. Gareth lived there, too, as he was mateless still. A couple of my wolves had gone ahead, calling for Christophe, the pack doctor. He lived not too far from the pack house with his wife and daughter. When we entered, shifting to our human forms, Christophe was already preparing the sofa with a crisp white sheet and had a medical table set up. Seemed a bit overkill, given the fact that as far as I'd scented, she had no open wounds of any kind.

Cody and Ash carried her in and placed her down on the sofa, letting her fall limp, an arm draping downwards and her fingers grazing the hardwood floor. I didn't know why, but it made my teeth grind. Waving off the strange sensation, I found myself staring at her limp form as one of my wolves handed me my cell. I dialed up Atlas, and he answered on the first ring.

"We found your runaway. Get to the Blood Moon pack house, asap." Then I hung up without waiting for his response. I knew he, Merrick, and Faust would be here shortly.

Christophe, sensing that she was stable after feeling for her pulse and for a fever, produced a large syringe from his medical bag. She was as limp as a dead body, and even from here, I could tell her pulse was weak. Whatever she'd gone through had been rough. Still, it was hard to have any sympathy for the daughter of one of the most despicable humans on the planet.

He approached her with the ease of a confident and practiced physician, and slowly injected a clear substance into her upper arm. I could smell the pungent odor from where I stood—liquid adrenaline. In seconds, the girl sprang from her position on the couch, white hair flying around her head. Every wolf in the room was crouched and ready to defend their alpha.

She was up and moving faster than any human woman would be able to move, crouched in a protective stance on the floor, facing me and my guards. As I looked Serenity Harker directly in her eyes, it was as if time, the world, and the universe ceased to exist. My blood ran boiling, and my teeth elongated from my gums. Claws replaced my fingernails as I partially shifted. It took tremendous restraint to refrain from letting my wolf free as I scented the air. More of that honey and floral scent hit me like a wrecking ball, making my cock harden instantly. I felt the need to fuck, to ruin, and to take.

She wouldn't look away. Couldn't. I couldn't either. The world grew dark on all sides, and the only light seemed to be emanating from her white blonde hair that cascaded down towards her hips. In my peripheral, I watched Gareth reach for her before she had the chance to utter a single snarl. He went for her neck, hand wrapping around her throat as he pushed her violently against the wall.

I moved before I realized what I was doing, going so fast, I was a blur. Soon, I had Gareth ripped away from Serenity and tossed across the room like he was nothing more than a sack of rocks. The wall cracked where he hit, and he instantly transformed into his wolf, shaking off the crumbling plaster and snarling. A growl ripped from my lips as the other wolves took giant steps backwards, eyes flitting between Gareth, the girl, and then me. I was breathing heavily, mind running a mile a minute, and I didn't know what to focus on.

Anger rolled through me as my brain kept flashing back to Gareth's hands on her pearly skin, squeezing around her windpipe. He was a loyal cousin and right-hand wolf, and yet I had the instant urge to rip that hand clean off. "What are you doing, Alpha?!" Christophe shouted, standing in the corner of the room, still clutching the syringe in his grip.

I snarled at him, and even coming from my still human mouth, it was menacing, enough that the doctor averted his eyes in submission. I instantly knew what was happening, but my mind was fighting tooth and nail to reject it. I fought hard to suppress the primal need coursing through my veins, the need to dominate, to claim. My eyes connected with the girl's again, those crimson and chocolate depths, so deep and dark and full of pain, sucking me in. I raged against anyone who dared put it there. Blood still coated that angelic face, but the fierceness that blazed from those eyes was enough to nearly bring me to my knees.

Instead, I prowled forward, squaring my shoulders and flexing my half shifted claws. Her eyes held mine the whole time. I was vaguely aware of the change in the air, the scent of vampires as three men entered the room. In the back of my mind, I knew Atlas, Merrick, and Faust had joined us in the pack house, but none of that mattered right now as I came nose to nose with Serenity Harker. I felt one word bubbling in my chest, ready to spill out like a snap of thunder.

I couldn't hold it in any longer. I couldn't fight it. I refused to fight it. After over one thousand years of waiting and hoping, I let myself utter the word, "Mate."

End Of Book One

AFTERWORD

Serenity's story only gets more insane from here! If you want more of this crazy world and these delectable creatures, follow the social media links below for updates and info on book two of Noc City.

YouTube: SheWrites
FB Reader Group, Penn's Peeps:
https://www.facebook.com/groups/373710066981813/
Instagram: @penncassidy

OTHER BOOKS BY PENN CASSIDY

Dead End (A Halloween Harem) with Madeline Fay

Printed in Great Britain
by Amazon